Resolve

A novel by
Neil Godbout

Bundoran Press

This is a work of fiction. The characters, incidents and dialogues are products of the author's imagination and are not to be construed as real. Any resemblance to actual events or persons, living or dead, is entirely coincidental.

Copyright © 2013 Neil Godbout

All rights reserved. No part of this book may be reproduced or transmitted in any form or by any means, electronic or mechanical, including photocopying, or recording, or by any information storage and retrieval system, without permission in writing from the publisher, except by a reviewer or academic who may quote brief passages in a review or critical study.

Cover Design: Virginia O'Dine

Printed in Canada
Published by Bundoran Press Publishing House
www.bundoranpress.com

Library and Archives Canada Cataloguing in Publication

Godbout, Neil, 1968-, author
Resolve / Neil Godbout.

(Broken guardian series)
ISBN 978-0-9880674-4-8 (pbk.)

I. Title. II. Series: Godbout, Neil, 1968- . Broken guardian series.

PS8613.O298R48 2013 C813'.6 C2013-903625-3

The Broken Guardian Series

Disintegrate
Dissolve
Resolve

For Claire and for the little people, Drayden and Myah.

"The second great law of thermodynamics involves a certain principle of irreversible action in Nature. It is thus shown that, although mechanical energy is indestructible, there is a universal tendency to its dissipation, which produces gradual augmentation and diffusion of heat, cessation of motion, and exhaustion of potential energy through the material universe. The result of this would be a state of universal rest and death…"

- Sir William Thomson, Lord Kelvin, 1862

The last piece (Amara)

Finally, something happens for me.

I thought I might possibly have to wait an entire human generation or two, until Sam's parents grew old and died, until Lily grew old and died, before Sam's link to humanity was finally severed and he would finish this farce permanently.

Now, I do not have to wait.

Lily is dead, killed in a genuine human accident, with no hand of intervention upon it by myself or anyone else.

What good fortune.

And now Sam has disappeared, at least to human eyes, but we all know where he is. He is gathering his core before spreading his darkness over all things, before making himself everywhere.

In all places, the lights shine brighter, in anticipation of being extinguished.

Dark seed (Max)

Sam's misfortune is my good luck.

Just as I am trying to figure out a way to kill Lily myself, more out of frustration because I could not have done such a thing, an accident happens. Well, an accident for her and her Sam. I can't believe my eyes looking down on it—there she is, lying on the grass, blood gushing out of her face, bone fragments from her nose thrust deep into her brain, killing her almost instantly.

Amazing.

I can't help myself. I'm dancing around the table, feeling alive again for the first time since…whenever. I'm feeling like I actually have a chance to get out of this ridiculous mess.

And then shit starts breaking down again, like it has been doing more and more, and I have to stop dancing and get back to work before the whole thing falls apart.

Now I remember the last time I was so happy. That was when Samael came upon the dark seed. I wasn't happy for very long. He just kept it to himself. If he'd have used it, he would have gotten what he wanted, destroying everyone and everything, and he'd have been happy and I'd have been happy and everything would have gone as it's supposed to. Well, it wouldn't have gone exactly like he planned but nobody gets everything they want. But no, he just took that beautiful dark seed and kept it to himself.

Stupid guardians.

They can't be trusted with anything of significance.

But what could I do? Nothing. Nothing but watch, which is what I've been doing since the very beginning. I just have to stay back and watch, keeping things together but not participating. Now, after so much time has passed, I am out of time. This construct is no longer sustainable and, as its caretaker, I am no longer able to maintain its viability.

It must be getting close now, because there is one guardian who feels me now and it is really confusing, especially to her little brain. Camille told Cameron what she feels because she had to tell someone and he has started to piece together some of what might be happening but he doesn't have all the pieces.

Bodie had a few pieces and he knew enough to help Amara pick up the dark seed and then make an excellent choice, giving the power to Sam, not that either of them really knew what they were doing.

Everybody has been looking at the clues and working towards their own conclusions, based on what they could perceive.

And now we're almost out of time and space and energy and they all have no idea what is truly at stake. Even if the guardians knew what was going on, they are still like me, weak and powerless. They have no influence on the final outcome. It is all up to him now.

Any time you're ready, Sam.

Just make it soon, please.

I'm dying and so is the mechanism.

Bodie's first question (Sam)

What did you lose when you murdered your sister?

Bodie asked me these questions when I had my vision of him but I didn't answer them. I ignored him. But now that I've run away, because Lily got herself killed in the most stupid of accidents, I'm scared of what I might do to myself and to everyone and everything. Who dies getting hit in the face with a baseball? It's a human thing, I guess, to die suddenly, like Lily did, standing there one second, hoping to field the ball and the next it's smashing into her face and crushing her nose into her brain. She would have liked to go like that, if she would have got to pick, dying in a way that was unexpected, that doesn't make sense.

There was no way I was even going to stop and talk to Crocodile. I would have stopped her or tried to and then who knows what would have happened. I felt Lily die, I saw right away that it wasn't some trick by Amara or Devi and then I was gone.

I mean gone. As in to the other side of the universe gone, about as far away from Earth and everybody as I can be.

And I'm already avoiding getting to work, addressing Bodie's questions, trying to find some meaning, something that makes sense, a way forward that doesn't involve me letting out that thing Amara put inside me then killing everybody. Even now—especially now—I have to find a way to fight that, to make sure it doesn't happen.

Okay, Bodie, I'm ready. Now I have no idea what the answer is but of course when the guardian of knowledge asks me a question like that, he already knows the answer and now he wants me to figure it out for myself, because maybe I'll come to some sort of revelation.

I think that's what he was after, anyway, but I can't focus on that. I have to concentrate on his words. If he thought this was important, then it must be important, and I waited too long to do it, to figure it out and then to really appreciate what it means.

I'm still human enough to understand the question and know I should have lost something but I don't feel the question inside. It's not a question that hits me in the gut. I just don't feel it. It's more like cracking the final level on a video game. It really annoys me and I want the answer, but only for my own satisfaction. I didn't feel much of anything about Sara. I didn't love her. And when it was time to kill her, I was scratching an itch, dealing with something that annoyed me, although she had the power to kill me and then everyone else.

The more I think about it, I'm not even sure the

question has an answer and that would be the way Bodie does things. Ask a question with no answer to point me in a direction, face me towards something he wants me to find. The question should be *What did I lose that I hadn't lost already?*

And there's the word that really describes me now.

Lost.

When Cindy was killed, Lily was lost and I went to find her and left her a beacon to find her way back to me. It helped but Missy was already there with her and that was what really got Lily through it, although Lily didn't tell me that until way later.

So Missy is here now and I let her do her thing, let her surround me, because I'm lost.

She doesn't talk, she won't even look at me, but she does make me hurt.

Maybe that's what I lost because I didn't feel like this when I had to kill Sara. I didn't feel anything except glad that I stopped her from killing everybody else because she was stupid and easily tricked by Amara.

But that's not fair.

How could Sara have known any different? She was so young and vulnerable. Amara told her everything she wanted to hear. She told Sara that I was mean and cruel and couldn't be trusted, which easily fit in to what Sara already knew and believed about me. I earned that because I tormented Sara her whole life. I didn't try very hard to save Sara, contain her somehow, until I could convince her she was being tricked. Scratch that—I made one quick effort to save Sara and then I gave up and dealt with her quick and easy, without a thought for her or for Mom and Dad.

I took the simple way out because I had the power to

do it. Just because you can do something doesn't make it right, Dad always says.

I wish Mom and Dad were here but just because I can be with them doesn't mean I should be.

I need to be as far away from living things as possible because I'm a threat to all of them.

If Missy wants to be here, that's her business. If I can stand Missy, maybe I can go back someday.

But since this happened to me, since I found out what I am, everybody is dying around me, and I can't take that anymore.

And now Lily's gone.

I felt it as soon as the baseball hit her, like a signal was sent out to find me and make me feel it.

I felt her brain drowning in blood. The electrical activity was scrambled like the static on a TV and then nothing. Her heart fluttered, waiting for someone to tell it what to do, and then it stopped, too.

And at that second, I made a choice.

There was Lily, lying on the ground dead. Of all the pathetic ways to go, I can't believe it.

Amara and Devi weren't there. No, it was just the little girl, Crocodile, standing over her with nothing but a white flower. She twirled it in her hands and sniffed it before looking at me. I could tell she was trying not to cry.

And beside her was Missy, the pain in her eyes sharp and cruel.

I could have killed both of them. Maybe I should have.

I couldn't. It wouldn't have changed anything.

I ran away and Missy followed me because that's what she's supposed to do. Is that it? Are we all just here to do what we're supposed to do? Am I just here to use that dark thing placed inside of me to kill everyone and destroy the universe?

There was Lily, lying on the ground, her face smashed, blood everywhere.

That's all I can see now.

That's all I feel I've lost.

Mysteries (Kathy)

The two cops come in and stand at the back of the hall as I look up from my notes to start the eulogy for Lily. One of them looks five years from retirement and 25 years past the time he would have been able to pass the physical to even get accepted into the police academy. He looks bored. I wish the other one looked bored, too, but he's younger, looks like he's in his early 30s, and he won't be so easy to lie to. He's young enough to still care and old enough to see through a liar.

He's already caught me in one lie and he can't catch me in another one. I won't let him, no matter what.

I stare at him long enough that more than a few people in the hall turn around to see who I'm looking at. He shouldn't be here but he's making a point and he doesn't care who sees him. He knows I know more about Lily than I'm saying. And that's the way it's going to stay.

I look down at my paper. My hands are still because standing in front of all these people is easy. Seeing Lily's body and her smashed-in face was hard. Finding those letters on her hard drive was hard. Hiding the computer and the keys to the storage locker was easy. Talking to the cops was easy until I got caught lying. Writing this eulogy was hard. Giving it will be easy. Lying again will go better. Finding out who Lily was will be hard but I'll do it, without these cops, well, that one cop, looking over my shoulder.

Not having Sam here is the hardest part.

Where is he? I need him and he's not here.

Now my hands start shaking. I push him out of my head and take a deep breath. I don't look up once as I read.

"We only had Lily for a short time but we all felt like we knew her forever. She came to Kelowna less than two years ago, to start Grade 12 at KLO. Her mother, Cindy, died in a car accident just a few months before graduation but Lily somehow found the strength to finish her courses and graduate with us. She left for the summer but came back in the fall and started classes at UBCO this year, where she was a top student. In her spare time, she sang with the Night Vision Beavers and they were becoming hugely popular on campus and in the city. When she wasn't singing or going to her classes or working at the library, she was playing sports—soccer and slo-pitch. She died doing her best and playing her best, just like she did everything else."

Now I look up at the young cop in the back. I ignore the rest of the sweet shit I had written. I'm angry at Lily for leaving me this mess and Sam for just leaving but I'm going to take out all of my anger on that guy in the back who's just doing his job and knows there's something wrong with this picture.

"Lily left behind 19 paintings and three sketch books but the cops took those two days ago," I tell him and the 150 people in this room, mostly students from KLO and UBCO, but also my family, Sam's parents, teachers and professors. "Apparently Lily had a past none of us knew about but the cops won't tell us what she did. So all of our memories, all of our good memories of Lily, are being challenged but they are our memories and we should treasure those. But now the cops are here, standing in the back…."

Now everyone turns around and there are angry whispers.

One of the Night Vision Beavers guys, I think it's Harrison, has to be stopped from getting up.

"…but they were just leaving. They've already talked to quite a few of us, asking us about Lily's past and they've taken all of her things she had at my place."

Both cops slip out of the room quickly. The old cop is shaking his head, the younger cop has put his head down in apology.

I wait until the door closes and the crowd turns back to me. I can feel the tension in the air and I'm vibrating. Somehow, I can still breathe and my voice seems to boom into the microphone in front of my face.

"It seems Lily and Cindy had a life before they came to Kelowna that none of us knew about but I don't care about that. She was my friend and I loved her. If she did things, bad things, before I knew her, I don't care. I saw her at her weakest and I saw her at her strongest. I believe in my friend and I always will."

I walk back down to sit with my mom. She squeezes my hand and whispers to me about how strong and loyal I am. I use that to stay focused on her and the rest of this service at Springfield Funeral Chapel. I have to stay sharp because there's lots for me to do.

I have to make sure the cops never find Lily's stuff.

And I have to find Sam, wherever he is.

No one has seen him since the night Lily died. His parents are a wreck. First Sara gets killed last October and now this. But he'll turn up, I know he will. He's going through his grief in his stupid writer, sensitive guy, way. I keep watching for him because I think he'll at least come to the service but he doesn't. I wonder if he knew about Lily's past and now is staying away to avoid being pulled into all of this.

I give out lots of hugs after the service and I just nod when people tell me I was courageous and good for me for telling the cops off like I did. Sam's dad tells me and my mom that he's going down to the detachment to file a complaint for harassment. I tell him I think that's a good idea.

For the next week, I'm a good girl. I go to work. I call Sam's parents every day to see if they've heard any news. Nothing. It's like he disappeared off the face of the Earth. He hasn't used his bank card. He has no extra clothes, no vehicle. His mom and dad go on TV and ask him to come home. I wonder if he's got himself mixed up in some of the stuff Lily and Cindy were mixed up in.

If this had happened a year ago, I'd be a wreck but me and Pete breaking up and spending so much time with Lily has changed me. I've taken Lily's talent of putting her life into boxes, delivering her life to certain people in pieces, like a character in a movie, and used it myself. It works pretty good, at least until I'm alone in my room at the end of the day. Then there's no one to talk to and I'm alone. It's so much at once—Lily getting killed in some stupid accident playing baseball and then Sam disappearing without a trace.

My head is pounding as I lie here on the couch, by myself in the quiet house, and now there's someone at the door.

I open it and there's wonderful young Corp. Jenson and his crusty old partner Sgt. Harding.

16

"Hi, Kathy," Jenson says, smiling. "We'd like to talk to you again about Lily if you have a minute."

Mom is at work and my sister is at school. They picked this time on purpose, knowing I'd be here alone. I have to be careful. Act cool and think smart, just like Lily always did when things were falling apart.

"I have to be at work in two hours and I have to get ready," I answer, acting bored and running my hand through my hair. "What can I tell you that I haven't told you already?"

"May we come in?" Harding asks. It's a sunny and warm afternoon. The old geezer is melting. There's sweat on his neck being soaked up by his shirt, which is too tight around his neck.

"Not without a warrant, Sgt. Harding," I answer, as firm and polite as I can, stepping forward and shutting the door behind me, forcing them to back down onto the top step so I'm now the same height as Jenson and taller than Harding.

"Kathy, please, call me Tom," Harding says, acting kind and fatherly.

"The last time I fell for that, you tricked me and then Corp. Jenson called me a liar, Sgt. Harding," I answer, keeping my voice level and stressing his title and name. "Ask me what you need to ask me and I'll decide if I need a lawyer."

"Aren't you curious about those letters Lily sent? Don't you want to know where Sam is? Don't you want to help his parents?" Jenson says, trying not to grit his teeth. We didn't get along the first time we met and it won't be any different this time. I have to be careful and not get mad like last time, when I accidentally let them know that I had read the letters Lily sent.

I take a deep breath.

"I am curious. I want to know where Sam is. I want to help his parents," I say in a flat voice.

"So help us, then," Jenson says. "When did you see those letters?"

"When I was cleaning up Lily's room, the day after she died. I had no idea she sent them. I thought they might be part of a novel or something she was working on. I just chucked them." I lie twice to his face.

"What else did you find in her room?"

"Nothing," I lie again. "You took all of her stuff. I don't have anything else of hers."

"Are you sure about that?" Harding asks, staring at me carefully. "Where's her laptop?"

I knew they would eventually ask about that so I'm ready.

"She kept a locker at the library at UBCO. It's not there?" I ask innocently.

"No, it's not. The library staff there told us she had a laptop but we can't find it for some reason," Jenson says. "When was the last time you saw her with it?"

"Sometimes it was on her desk in her room, sometimes it wasn't. I don't know. Maybe a few weeks ago?"

Jenson keeps staring at me. Harding looks down and away, cooking in the sun.

"I'm sorry your friend is not who you thought she was," Harding starts, his voice soft and sympathetic. "Look at it from our perspective. Lily sent out letters with intimate details about four murders, two of which likely happened before she was born. We can't find birth records in Canada for her, her mother or her father. Her former boyfriend is missing. And you admit to reading those letters but say you took nothing else out of her room."

"I spent 10 minutes cleaning the papers off her desk and emptying her waste basket," I say, my voice breaking. "I couldn't do anymore."

I chew my lip and look away, wiping my eyes. My grief is sincere. Everything else is bullshit. Jenson knows it.

"I don't believe you, Kathy," he says, angrily but not raising his voice. "I think you have her laptop and some other things in your bedroom right now."

"I don't," I moan, letting my tears come. I can feel my face getting hot. "I told you guys I don't. Why don't you believe me? I'm sorry I lied about the letters but I didn't know what they were or what they meant. I lost my best friend and now another friend is missing. I'm confused and I don't know what to do."

They must teach them at police school not to look away when people are crying because they are both studying me carefully. I wipe my eyes again. At least, I'm not lying anymore. The laptop is not here, that's for sure. They have the rest—the clothes, the art, her school stuff.

"So if we got a warrant and came back and searched your place, we wouldn't find anything else of Lily's?"

"No, nothing," I sniff.

"No pictures of her mom or dad? Contact information for her dad or the rest of her family? Nothing at all?" Harding asks.

I look at both of them and something about Lily occurs to me. She never called Cindy her mom. She called her Cindy. Bodie was Bodie, not Dad. Who was Cindy? Where is Bodie now? These are questions for me to answer. I was Lily's friend, or at least I thought I was. I wish she was here. She would know what to do, what to say to get these cops to back off.

19

"Why are you guys spending so much time on the letters a dead girl sent to some people, anyway?" I demand, getting my confidence back.

Harding looks at Jenson and Jenson looks away for a second.

"See, your partner thinks it's a waste of time, too," I tell Jenson, motioning at Harding. "Don't you have bad guys to catch, Corp. Jenson? Maybe she you should stop wasting your time on a dead girl who maybe Googled some people and then pulled a prank on them?"

"That prank hurt those people," Jenson stiffens his jaw. "Their loved ones are dead."

"And so's my friend and another one is missing. That's the case I'd like you guys to work on. Where the hell did Sam Gardner go? His parents lost their daughter in a car accident last fall and now their son has been missing for more than a week. Go find him. Please."

I'm talking firmly at them, giving them each a hard stare because they need to get out of here. I'm going to fall apart any minute, especially playing the Sam card to these jerks.

Harding steps back but Jenson doesn't move.

"Thank you for your time," Harding says.

Jenson just stares at me and then follows his partner to the car without a word.

I don't watch them leave. I get inside as fast as I can and slam the door. I can barely breathe.

Lily's dead. Sam's gone and maybe dead, too.

I cry my way through my shower but I'm better as I get dressed, do my hair and slip on some makeup. The routine of getting ready for work calms me down.

Inside my purse are Lily's keys, jingling as I walk to the bus stop. I don't work for three days after tonight so

I'll have some time to do my own police work, to find out what these keys are and what else is on that laptop, other than those four letters that were on the desktop.

I show up just in time for the bus and take a seat right at the back. I pull the keys out and study them again.

There is a safety deposit box key but I have no idea which bank to go to and there's nothing on the key to help me figure it out. The only reason I know it's a safety deposit key is because I looked it up on Google images. I'll have to look for some financial records on Lily's laptop so I can find out where to go with this. There's the storage locker key and I know that because it says Kelowna Self-Storage right on it. There are two more keys that look like just regular keys for locks of some sort. No idea what those could be for.

I put them back into my purse and close it.

I need to be bubbly sexy Kathy at the pub. I make more money that way. In my room tonight, I'll crack open that laptop and see what's inside, other than those four horrible letters. I'm the one that's going to find out what's going on, not those cops.

Just after (Missy)

I like Sam, I really do.

He's a nice boy when he wants to be and he tries so hard to do the right thing.

After Lily is hit in the face by that ball, Sam knows she's dead before she hits the ground.

And I feel Sam's hurting like no other I've ever felt before, not even with Amara or Lily herself. His suffering starts with a few seconds of disbelief and then his physical form is gone. His parents are at the Dairy Queen having soft vanilla ice cream and he is at home alone, which is a good thing.

He looks from high overhead as Lily's teammates rush to her and then he takes off, away from the Earth, away from this solar system, away even from this galaxy. There's nowhere he can run from me, of course, but I'm scared. I know Cameron told me he will accept me in the end but that doesn't stop me from being nervous.

He's hurt me twice already and I didn't like that.

He's gathered himself in a pulsar on the far side of the universe.

What a dummy.

Time slows down here because of the gravity but it still runs at the same speed everywhere else.

I tell him that, except for the part about being a dummy.

He glares at me.

I hope I haven't made a big mistake.

Letter Number One (Lily)

Dear Ms. Brenner,

This is going to be a difficult and disturbing letter to receive for you so let me apologize from the very beginning. I will try to explain everything I can. I know you will probably have questions and wish to contact me. It's about your brother Jeff and how he died.

My grandmother's name was Cynthia but sometimes she called herself Cindy. I have her diary and she specifically asked me to have it after she passed away. I just put it in my bookshelf and left it there as a nice keepsake. I loved her very much. She was a strong lady and she inspired me to be the same.

Last month, I finally took her diary down and start-ed reading it. It's all in one big leather book and it has the years 1966 to 1970 in it. Apparently she didn't keep a diary before or after that, or at least one that's been found. She was in her 20s then and living in Vancouver.

So I was going through my grandmother's diary and I couldn't believe what I was reading. She said she killed a man and she put down his name and when it happened. I think that's your brother.

I'm so sorry but I thought I should tell you because I doubt if you know what happened to him. She died earlier this year and no one in the family ever knew. I'm sorry for what she did. She wrote that she did it because she didn't want him to know who she really was. I don't know what that means. My grandma was running from bad people, she says, and she thought your brother knew too much and might tell on her.

I don't know what happens to bodies after such a long time or if it's still there but she says his body was left in the water, close to Siwash Rock at Stanley Park.

I wanted to tell you because he must have just dis-appeared to you, without a trace. I looked it up in the newspaper archive and it said he was last seen leaving the Retinal Circus club at 2:30 a.m. on May 12, 1968 with an attractive blonde woman.

That was my grandmother.

They went to Stanley Park and that's where he was killed.

I'm so sorry.

I burned my grandmother's diary that night I read about your brother but I couldn't forget him and I couldn't stop thinking about his family so I did some research at the library and on Google and I found you.

I hope the police and the divers can still find him and you can maybe give him a proper burial.
Lily
Kelowna, BC

Bodie's second question (Sam)

What did you lose when you attempted to murder Lily?
Which time?

When I sat with her crystal essence on the beach, thinking all I had to do was break it apart because she was trapped in it and that would kill her? Or a few minutes after that, when I held her hand and passed it to Crocodile, that sweet little girl who is actually the guardian of death and who all living things must pass through to get to wherever the dead go? I wanted her dead that time, too.

The easy answer is that both of those times I was under Amara's control but that opens up some problems for me, which I'm sure is exactly what Bodie wanted me to realize.

Because if Lily was able to come up with a way to stay alive and get me back from Amara, why didn't I do the same for Sara? Wouldn't it have been easier for Lily to kill me, just like it was easier for me to kill Sara? Problem solved.

Lily could have killed me right then and all this would have been fixed. She would have had to kill Sara eventually, too, but two teens from Kelowna would have been a small price to pay to save all the other living things in existence.

Why didn't she do it?

I know the answer to that one.

Because she loved me.

Because she believed I was better than what Amara wanted me to be, because she believed in the human spirit so much that she was sure I could find a way to control my power.

So then what did I lose, when I tried to kill Lily, not once but twice?

Faith in Lily, trust in me and her to do the right thing, I guess.

I'd say confidence but I don't think I ever had it. The only time I've ever felt confident is when I've used my power, because it's so much bigger than me. When I use it, I feel I can do anything I want, whenever I want, but when I do that, everything goes wrong, even when I have the best of intentions.

The real answer is what hurts the most and I know this is what Bodie wanted me to face.

I lost hope.

And I never got it back.

I couldn't believe skinny little Sam Gardner, the chosen one destined to bring about the destruction of the universe, could actually be what Lily saw. I couldn't believe that I was actually bigger than this power of mine and that I could beat it with my human spirit. The only thing I could see in myself was what Amara saw—a helpless tool that would follow orders, claiming all along I had no choice.

I thought Lily had given up hope by becoming completely human but now I wonder if I got that wrong. Maybe it was a message for me, to eventually figure out, something where she had to show me, and not just tell me, that I could do the same.

Take control by giving up the power.

I was so desperate to be something more, someone

who could make a difference, that I thought I had to keep this thing Amara made in me. Instead, I could have been something more by rejecting it, by turning the power on itself.

But I don't think it works that way. There's no way I could just chop it off from myself, especially since I don't have a heart anymore, after I gave it to Crocodile.

So then what?

Give it back to Amara? She'll just infect someone else with it.

Give it to Devi?

If there's anyone who might be able to control it, it's her. She is the guardian of control, after all. She could wrap it in a box and put it away. If there's one thing I learned from her, it's that control isn't about using power, it's about not using the power you have. The more you have to use power, the more you've lost control of the situation.

True control is about being so above the situation that whatever happens doesn't matter, you'll adjust. Use power in short little bursts, push players gently one way or another, and let their momentum carry them the rest of the way. Make them think it was their idea all along and that they're in control, when really it's her all along, quietly tugging on invisible strings.

That's what she's been doing the whole time.

I'm not sure I can trust her. I'm not sure the answer is to pass off this power and this responsibility. I had plenty of chances to do it but now, with Lily gone, I don't think that's what I have to do. I think I have to face this by myself, my power against the little bit of human that might be left in me.

Pretty crappy odds.

Maybe I should talk to Devi, anyway, to explore all my options.

I'd like to ask Lily but she's gone.

Missy moves closer.

Lily's gone.

I get a few minutes of what feels like understanding and clarity, some space where I can think about all of this and what I should do next. When I do, Missy steps back and I can breathe. But whenever I start thinking about the questions Bodie gave me, I always end up back here, with the one fact I can't escape.

Lily's gone.

Missy puts her arms around me and everything disappears except for those two words.

Lily's gone.

Lilith (Kathy)

I'm paranoid packing this laptop home. I've been looking over my shoulder every five seconds, to make sure no one is watching me. I couldn't be looking or acting more guilty if I tried.

I get off the bus and walk fast and nervous up the street to my place, half-expecting one of those cops to jump out of the bushes but nothing happens. It's after midnight and it's warm so I'm sweating and breathing too fast. My hands are shaking but I get the key into the door and let myself in.

I stop in the hallway, listening to make sure Mom and Jill aren't up. I tiptoe downstairs but instead of going into my room, I go into Lily's old room and close the door. Between the cops and Mom, it's been cleaned out so good that it's back to the spare room it was before Lily came to stay with us, after Sara was killed in the car accident. I unpack the laptop from the case and turn it on. I prop up the pillows against the wall and sit down on the bed, my back against them, sighing.

What am I doing?

Why don't I just give the keys and the laptop to the cops?

Couldn't I go to jail for withholding evidence or something?

I'm thirsty. I should have brought a beer down with me.

Except for those four strange and horrible letters, the only thing on the desktop is a folder called My Stuff.

I click open My Stuff.

There is a folder called Lilith. That's Lily's full name, I guess. I had never thought about it.

Beside the Lilith folder, there are two loose files. Their names make me take a sharp breath. I look around the room and wish I had left more than just the lamp on the desk on.

One says "Read Me Sam" and the other says "Read Me Kathy."

I close my eyes and try to slow my heart down, my head against the wall.

Where are you, Sam? Why aren't you here to help me with this?

Lily died and he ran away. I knew he wasn't over her but how could he be gone for so long and not call his parents who are so worried? It's been 12 days now.

He's not here and who knows when he'll be back. The cops think something happened to him because of those letters Lily wrote and I can't help but think they're right. I'd like to think that Sam was as much in the dark about

Lily as I was but that's not what it looks like. I open my eyes and stare at the door.

I thought I might be falling in love with Sam, not for the first time, this spring but now that he's not here, I know I wasn't. I don't miss him as much as I should. He was always distant to me, holding back, and I just can't have that. I put myself out there and I can't be with any guy who doesn't do the same. I learned that the hard way with Pete. Tonight, I flirted shamelessly while serving drinks and pocketing my tips. There were at least five or six guys who I could have taken home but I haven't been with anyone since Pete, not that I haven't been tempted. Too picky, Lily would say.

That makes me smile a little and I can look down at the laptop and click the file I'm supposed to read. The document opens.

My dearest Kathy,

If it's you reading this, I hope you read one or all of the four letters on the desktop and called Sam immediately. He knows about my past and will know what to do. If you are reading this now, Kathy, and Sam is available to help you, stop and find him, no matter what's happened. Sadly, I suspect that if you are reading this, I am dead and Sam has disappeared, not wanting to be part of any more deaths—Cindy, Sara and now me. It also means you may have hidden this laptop from the police and become complicit in my crimes and, among so many other things in my life, I am sorry for that, too.

As you likely already have concluded, I have a past I never told you about but it's much deeper than that. I know you will have a difficult time believing this but I have been alive for many hundreds of years, always as a 17-year-old, until very recently, when I was able to complete my transformation into a human being and start aging properly. I was present at the deaths of all four of the people in those letters and I killed Jeff, Rachel and Gary myself. I'm so sorry for that, which is why I finally wrote those letters, but, of course I couldn't tell them I was 17 years old in 1968 and in 1976, too. The letters are correct about killing them for a reason. Those four people were all able to tell that Cindy and I looked human but that we were different for some reason. We were scared that these people who could somehow tell we weren't human would alert the ones like us who wanted to find Cindy and me to kill us.

So I killed Jeff, Rachel and Gary. Cindy killed David. It was self-defence or self-preservation (or at least that's what we told ourselves it was) and it was wrong. I know that and I could never atone for it.

And then Cindy died and I just couldn't do it anymore, running and hiding, so I became human, so I could be closer to Sam, and live and die properly, but then we broke up and it all seemed like a waste at first. Thanks to you, I realized I had a lot to live for but I also had to take responsibility for my terrible crimes, at least in some small way, which is why I wrote the letters. I hope I can tell you these things in person, after the police come to question me, but if you are reading this, something has happened to me.

So if Sam has gone as well, then it's just you, Kathy, and you are reading part of my last will and testament. I know my story is crazy but you know I wouldn't lie to you with so stupid a lie if it wasn't true. Even if you don't believe me right now, you will. Just follow the instructions below and you'll see for yourself.

You are the executrix of my estate. Inside the My Stuff

folder, you will find the contact information for Gilles Parenteau, my lawyer in Paris. He knows the location of my holdings around the world and will assist you in the international legal complexities surrounding them and he is aware of my true identity. He also holds my legal will, which states how I wish my possessions to be distributed.

There is an account in your name at Valley First Credit Union downtown with $100,000 dollars cash in it, perhaps a bit more now with the little bit of interest it is accumulating. That will provide you with enough funds to investigate my identity further, if you so choose, and to visit M. Parenteau in Paris.

I hope you have also kept my keys. One of the keys is for safety deposit box number 1566 at the same branch of Valley First Credit Union. Inside, you will find documents to give to M. Parenteau with legal instructions for him and some small mementos and other items I want you to have.

I'm sorry I have burdened you with this, Kathy. I have done horrible things to save myself and the ones I loved but I am not a horrible person. Since I met you, I never wanted to be anything more than the Lily you saw in me. Despite the lies I told you and the past I couldn't reveal to you, I hope you can believe how much I loved you.

Your loyal friend always,

Lily

I read it five or six times, each time ignoring one part so I can digest another because it's too big to take it all in. There's the part about being hundreds of years old (*How many hundreds? Where did she live? What is she?*) and being on the run from others like her (*Why? What did she and Cindy do? Would they want to hurt me or Sam?*) is crazy and impossible but even with all of the questions, it just might be true when it comes to Lily.

She's a murderer.

She killed three people. She killed a little girl.

I don't know how to connect that to Lily, even though she's saying she did it.

But the letters—what about them?

She believes she killed those people and helped Cindy kill the other one.

It doesn't make sense for Cindy or Lily.

I might even believe they're creatures that are hundreds of years old and don't age and are able to look and act like human beings.

I can't believe they killed people while they were hiding.

It makes no sense at all.

But she wants me to find out the truth for myself. She left me all that money and instructions to find her lawyer.

Now I'm clicking through the Lilith folder.

Along with the address and phone number to the Paris lawyer, there are street and web addresses to banks in Europe, Eastern Canada, the U.S., the Middle East, Russia and Australia with account numbers attached to them.

How much money does she have?

Why does she have it hidden all over the world?

There is also the address to Kelowna Self Storage. She must have put her extra things there so that must be what one of the keys is for. So one of the keys is for the safety deposit box and another is for the storage locker. I wonder what the other keys are for? Could be something important or it just could be something simple and not important, like her locker at school or something like that.

The rest of the stuff is just homework and other school stuff.

There are no links in her browser and no e-mail addresses I can use. There's some geek who could probably find deleted emails and the deleted history in her browser but that geek's name is Sam. The same kind of geek who could also do it works with the cops and that's not going to happen, especially now, after reading and seeing all this.

I have a headache and I can't stop yawning. My brain is spinning but I'm so tired. I close the laptop and lie down without shutting off the lamp. I only sleep for a few hours and I have dreams where people wearing disguises are chasing me with guns and knives. The shower helps wash them away. I almost feel like myself after my makeup and some fresh clothes are on.

I take a deep breath, put on my happy face and head into the kitchen for breakfast with Mom.

"Morning, pumpkin," she says, cheerfully. She finishes pouring her coffee and comes to give me a hug. "You slept in Lily's room last night?"

Funny how Lily only lived with us for eight months and the spare room downstairs became Lily's room.

"Yeah," I say, hugging her back. "Can I have some coffee, too, Mom? There's something I need to ask you."

"Sure, sure," she answers, fishing for a mug in the cupboard. "Triple, triple?"

"Yes, please," I say, grabbing the cream from the fridge.

Mom adds three spoons of sugar. I add the cream, stirring quickly.

"I heard you getting up so I made an extra egg and toast," she points to the plate on the counter.

Normally, I'd take that but my stomach does a flip when I see it. I head to the pantry and pull out the plastic wrap.

"No thanks, Mom. I'll leave it for Jill. I really need to talk to you about something, instead. Do you have a few minutes before work? Actually, I'd like a ride downtown."

She glances at her watch while I pop the plate in the fridge. We sit at the kitchen table together.

"Sure, pumpkin, but I can't be late. I have a meeting with the mayor and the city manager this morning."

"I don't want to make you late," I protest.

"I meet the mayor and the city manager all the time. Same old administrative bullshit. C'mon, what's up?"

Ever since Mom became finance manager at city hall last year, she's been super busy. She still gives me and Jill lots of love but she's really focused with her time. Things always need to be moving forward quickly and efficiently. If I'm going to talk about this with her, I need to put it in a nutshell but I have to leave out some important parts.

"Mom, I saw those letters Lily wrote the night before the police came, after she was killed. I hid her laptop and her keys from them," I tell her as straightforward as I can.

She stares at me, digesting what I've told her.

"Why did you do that?" she asks, her voice and face now tight. "You may have just made yourself an accomplice in a crime. I believed you when you said you didn't know where the laptop was. What are you hiding?"

She looks away, already jumping ahead.

"I need to call Alex. We need a cover story that you found it in a closet somewhere."

"Mom, please, Mom, I don't need a lawyer," I say, taking her hand on the table and squeezing it. My voice cracks but I hold it together. "I just need you to listen first."

Her stare is cool. She doesn't answer but at least I have her attention.

"I hid her laptop in my locker on campus and brought

it home only last night to look at it. There was a note to me in it that explains those letters she wrote. She wrote that I'm in charge of her will. I have to go to Valley First Credit Union today and pick up some money she left me in a bank account and then I have to go to Paris to meet her lawyer."

Mom takes a big swallow of coffee.

"Let's talk in the car," she says, getting up and pouring the rest in the sink.

I scramble to keep up, stuffing my feet into sneakers and running into the garage. The car is already running and the door is open.

As I put my seatbelt on, she backs up and clicks the garage door remote once we're clear. She slips the car into drive and we're moving quickly down the street.

"What did she say in the note? Lily can't be guilty of those crimes, because she could only be alive for one of them and she would have been a preschooler, but they could have been committed by her father, who did not come to her funeral and is now nowhere to be found," Mom says, analyzing the situation with what she knows. "The police told me they have no birth records for Lily and her identification was forged. Same with her mother."

"Mom, she didn't explain any of that but she did say that she feels responsible so maybe it was her dad but she doesn't say," I look at her but she's keeping her eyes locked on the road. If Mom wants to blame Bodie for this, I'll go with that. It's the answer that makes the most sense. Lily didn't mention Bodie in her note to me.

"I still don't like that you hid the laptop and lied to the police. And what are these keys you have?" she says, speeding through a yellow light.

"They were on her desk with the laptop so I just

grabbed them. One of them is a key to a safety deposit box at Valley First. There's some documents in there I need to take to her lawyer."

"In Paris. France, I presume, and not Texas. How much money did she leave you to do this?"

I answer quickly so I don't lie.

"$100,000."

Mom blows out some air sharply through her lips, shaking her head.

"So let me get this straight. You've been left a shitload of money by a girl with no identity, whose mother also had no identity but is now dead and whose father is likely a murderer and can't be found. You withheld evidence from a police investigation into four murders that Lily had intimate knowledge of and now you want to take this money, who knows where it came from, and head halfway around the world to meet a lawyer. Do you have any idea what you're getting into, Kathryn? Do you have any idea what kind of people you might be dealing with?"

She hasn't raised her voice but her knuckles are white on the steering wheel and her jaw underneath her ear has started to twitch.

"I have no idea, mom, but Lily wasn't just a girl, she was my best friend and I know she wouldn't have asked me to do this if she thought I could get hurt," I answer as best I can. "I wish Sam was here."

I finally lose it and cover my face with my hands, my whole body shaking as I cry.

Her hand squeezes my shoulder.

"We'll be at Valley First in a minute, pumpkin, and I'll drop you off. Do your banking and then text me. I should be out of my meeting by then and we'll grab an early lunch. I'll call Alex in the meantime and maybe he can join us."

I pull myself together as she glides to a stop in front of the credit union. She hands me a tissue from her purse.

"Do you think Sam knew more about Lily?" she asks, her voice more gentle now.

"I know he did. Lily said so in her note to me. She said I should get him to help me."

"And now he's missing, too," she says, a sharp crease of concern on her forehead. "The more I hear about this, the worse it gets."

She's unfastened her seatbelt to hug me.

"I have to go, pumpkin," she squeezes then quickly lets me go. "Text me when you're ready for lunch. Bring whatever is in that safety deposit box and we'll look at it together then."

"Okay, mom," I answer, nodding and then getting out of the car as fast as I can. She waves her hand and smiles as best she can before speeding down the street towards the lake and city hall.

I turn towards the door at Valley First but only take one step forward. Not open until 930. Mom dropped me off 45 minutes early. The street is not too busy yet so I easily walk across to the Safeway. There's a Starbucks inside where I can grab a coffee and think about all of this and what mom said.

I sit with my coffee and stare at the door to the credit union.

Lily's death was a complete accident, there's no doubt about that. But is Sam's disappearance because he's feeling sorry for himself or because he's hiding from the people looking for Lily or because he's already been caught by them for knowing too much?

Mom's right. I have no idea what I'm getting into.

I know Lily wouldn't ask me to do something where I could get hurt but then why did she tell Sam? Did she put him in danger by telling him?

I catch myself turning to see if anyone's watching me but I'm alone except for the two people behind the Starbucks counter, and then there are a few shoppers and the Safeway workers. I stare at the credit union door again.

I'm in too deep already. I have to find out for myself about Lily and maybe I'll even find out where Sam might be in the process. I don't believe something happened to him. He's just hiding out somewhere, feeling sorry for himself and maybe really scared. I have to believe that. I couldn't take losing my two best friends in one shot like that.

That's why I can't let go of this. It's the last thing of Lily I have and now there's a lot more to it than I could ever have guessed. I'm curious and confused about what she says she and Cindy were. I want to understand her and I believe her when she said I was her best friend. I never had a friend like her and I'm going to be loyal to her, even now that I'm finding out all of this extra stuff about her.

I pull her keys out of my purse. After doing the banking stuff and getting the papers out of the safety deposit box, I'm going to the self-storage place and seeing what she kept there. Once I see all of that stuff, I'll know more about what I'm getting into. Then I'll decide when, or if, I'm going to Paris.

I've only taken a few sips of my mocha and it's now lukewarm. I drink it quickly. There are two people waiting on the sidewalk now in front of the credit union. It must be almost time for them to open.

I was so deep in my thoughts and so focused on across

the street that I didn't notice a blind man had sat down at the table next to me, propping his white cane up against the table. He's facing in my direction but I can't tell if he's looking at me behind those dark glasses. Not that he'd be looking at me if he's blind, I scold myself for taking this long to figure out the obvious. He's got coffee in his mug. He's here for a while. I take a deep breath and I'm on my feet and outside. It's time to find out what's going on.

Not long after (Missy)

Well, he's finally figured some of it out, at least.

It's not like he has much choice or anything.

If you're going to have that kind of power, bad things are going to happen around you because you're going to do things and not appreciate what it means until it's too late. That's what Cam said and I believe it.

It's the human in him and the goodness in him that is causing all of this grief. He just wants to do the right thing and make things better. It's the belief that things get better—Cam calls it the myth of progress—that is so human. And by trying to make things better, they so often make things worse but they still keep trying. Cam apologized to some guy whose name I can't remember for quoting his ideas on this and then said Sam will always do the right thing, right after he's exhausted every other possibility.

Even I get that joke.

Sam has finally seen the pattern—Cindy, Cherry, Ruby, Dan, Kyle, Sara and now Lily. Even Bodie. It all goes back to him.

And he's finally listening to Lily. She told him before she died.

He's using his power on himself. I'm here and he's

hurting like he should.

Cam should come by and see Sam pretty soon. Then we'll get somewhere.

Letter Number Two (Lily)

Dear Mr. And Mrs. Henderson,

This letter will come as a terrible shock to you, nearly 40 years after you lost Rachel, but I know neither of you have been at peace since her death. You want answers and I'm writing to give you as many as I can.

I was there when Rachel died. It was my mother who killed her.

She didn't die in the fall from the top of the building. Her neck was broken first. My mother grabbed her from behind and Rachel didn't even have time to be scared. We took her onto the roof and dropped her into the alley. What a terrible way to leave such a beautiful girl.

We did it on purpose and we did it because we were scared that your daughter knew something about us she shouldn't. We were running from people who wanted to hurt us and we put our safety above Rachel's life. I wish we had had the courage to face those who wanted to find us but we didn't.

Your little girl didn't suffer, I swear it, but I know you knew it was us and you wanted justice, so we should pay for our terrible crime. I'm so sorry I hurt you like this. We were both so scared and it tore us up inside to do it and now that my mother is gone, I have to tell you. I know I don't deserve to be forgiven but I do know you deserve to know what really happened to Rachel, which is why I'm writing to you. She was a beautiful little girl who deserved much better than to meet me and my mother.

I know telling the truth now will open so many wounds but I hope you will heal better now, knowing you didn't fail her and that it wasn't your fault. I accept that blame completely, for myself and my mother. I am not deserving of any forgiveness but I write to you in hopes that one day I can be.

Lily
Kelowna, BC, CANADA

Bodie's third question (Sam)

What did you lose when you gave your beating heart to Camille?

I gave her the wrong thing that day on the beach, that's for sure.

I could have put my power into that dead heart but instead I put my human self. Why did I do that? How stupid could I be? It would have made so much more sense to ditch my power, although I'm not sure if I could have done it. How do you use power to get rid of it?

I don't think Camille can do trades so I can get my heart back. And I don't think I can give her my power without including the rest of me in the package. I'd have to go to her like Bodie did, as a complete surrender.

But wait, she's death. Wouldn't she just take the power and do what comes naturally, do what she is?

Maybe not.

Probably not.

She doesn't work that way.

She doesn't cause death, she is death. She's just the last stop in the process, she doesn't initiate it, at least I don't think so. Like with Lily, on the beach, she can't reach out and grab the person, they have to be brought to her. She's not the king, she's just the executioner.

I can hear Lily now and I can see Bodie nodding.

You find it so easy to analyze others but you seem unable to apply your insight to yourself.

And I know my answer to that now.

I'm just trying to be human but I'm not. Not anymore.

And I know what I lost, to answer the full question Bodie gave me.

I gave away what I thought for the longest time was my humanity, my human self, and now I'm this power and I'm like a guardian and I can live forever and my body is just a shell.

Wrong. Completely wrong.

The longer I'm outside of my body, the more I realize it.

I gave away my beating heart but that's all. It's not a symbol of what I am. It's just a heart. I gave it the power to beat on its own. I gave it the potential of life, which is what the little girl loved so much about it. I took something broken and I fixed it. That's important.

Maybe that means she might still have it but it doesn't matter. I don't need my heart to be human. It's like Lily herself once said, it's the effort to be human, to be moral, to be good, that's what counts.

A person who receives a heart transplant doesn't stop being human. It just means they have a machine inside their chest to pump the blood through their body. That human part is tied up in my thoughts, or in my "notions of self-consciousness" as Bodie would say.

A serial killer has a beating heart and a brain but gives up his humanity with his actions.

I've killed guardians. I've killed my sister. Lily killed humans and guardians.

How did she get past that?

She found a way back.

She lost the good part of herself but it wasn't lost forever. She got it back.

Well, she got it back for a short time.

And then she was gone.

And she's not coming back.

But Missy is back.

I hold her as hard as I can because there's nothing else to hold.

Peeking behind the curtain (Kathy)

After I give the safety deposit box key to the cheerful lady behind the desk, she gets me to sign a card. She asks me for my driver's licence, tapping the numbers into the computer, before she leads me into the vault. She puts my key and her key into one of the large drawers, then pulls it out, gasping a little. I jump to help her. It is surprisingly heavy.

"Must have a rock collection in here," the lady—Sophie it says on her tag pinned to her Valley First Credit Union vest—puffs.

"Yeah, must be," I answer, adjusting my grip.

We carry the drawer into a small room next to the vault and put it on a table attached to a wall. The room is the size of a closet with only a chair. Sophie is already leaving the room.

"I'll leave you with that," she smiles."Call me when you're done."

She shuts the door.

The drawer is two feet long but only four inches high and just wide enough to hold papers.

I unclasp the drawer on its side and open it length-wise.

Well, that's why it's so heavy.

I thought solid gold bricks only existed in the movies but here are two of them, blinking at me under the fluorescent lights. I try to pick one up with one hand and quickly slide my other hand underneath or I'll drop it. I place it on the table beside the drawer and stack the other gold brick on top. They both have a stamp on top that says LBMA.

I look up at the ceiling, paranoid someone's watching but there are only the lights. The whole room is painted in a dull off-white.

I concentrate real hard to slow my breathing. Gold bars. Who knows how much they're worth? But I can't get distracted.

I ignore the gold bars because there will be time to find out what they're worth later. I can't even guess. The coffees, the one at home and the one at Starbucks, with no breakfast have given me a headache. I blink and concentrate on the drawer.

There is a large business envelope. I pull it out. It's sealed shut and it has the name of the lawyer in Paris on the front, his address, his phone number and his email. I put the envelope on the chair.

Underneath that is just a stack of papers, each one protected inside a clear plastic holder. Most of them don't make sense to me but the ones in English say "treasury" on them and come from Canada, the U.S., England and Australia. Most of them say $50 or $100 dollars on them but they look very old. I put them on top of the gold bars.

There are some old coins, also in plastic collector wrappers. I don't even bother to study them. I just put them with the other stuff.

The last thing inside is a small piece of paper, torn from a notepad.

It says "Sam – 027-105872" and underneath that it says "Kathy – 027-105873."

Must be the account number. She set up an account for Sam, too. I bet he was her first choice to handle all of this stuff and I was the backup. Makes sense. I open my purse and put the paper inside a zippered compartment so I won't lose it.

I put the coins back in and place the stack of papers on top. The gold bars go last and I lay them carefully. I close the drawer and clasp it, double-checking to make sure it won't open. I have no idea what most people keep in their safety deposit boxes but I bet it's not gold bars.

I open the door but stand there, waiting for the lady to see me, not letting the drawer out of my sight until it's locked up in the vault again, looking safe and anonymous with all of the other safety deposit boxes around it. After we're done, I take the envelope and hold it as casually as I can, against my hip.

"Is there anything else I can help you with?" she asks.

"Yes, please," I say. "I would like to withdraw $50 from my account here."

"We can do that. Follow me," she smiles in answer and leads me to the other side of the branch where the customer service counters are.

"This is Evelyn, she can help you from here. Have a good day," she smiles again.

"I will and thank you for your lifting help," I say, turning on that charm Mom always told me will get me ahead in life.

"You're welcome," Sophie nods, laughs pleasantly, and walks away.

Evelyn is not quite so friendly. She pushes a slip of paper across the counter.

"Name and account number, please."

I take out the piece of paper from my purse and write the number down, with my name, and push it back to her.

"And an account balance, please," I ask politely.

"Certainly," she answers, very business-like. "May I have some identification, please?"

I put the account paper back in its safe place in my purse and pull out my driver's licence.

Evelyn checks it carefully, looking at it then studying my face, before she writes down the licence number on the slip of paper with my name. She hands it back.

Now her fingers are flying across the keyboard, tapping in my name and the numbers.

A small machine spits out some paper.

"Sign, please," she puts it in front of me.

I scribble my name. Evelyn takes it away, pulls it apart and tucks the white copy in a drawer, pulling one $50 bill out of the same drawer. She writes the balance on the yellow copy and hands me the cash.

"Thanks," I say, careful not to look at the paper yet, making eye contact with Evelyn.

"You have a good day," Evelyn says, her voice friendly but no smile on her face.

"I will," I answer, already walking away, the money and paper held tight in my right hand.

I don't look until I get outside.

$50 bill, all red and crisp with a picture of Mackenzie King, prime minister of Canada from 1935 to 1948 (I paid too much attention in social studies).

Yellow paper with information about my $50 withdrawal, the account number and my signature. On the other side are Evelyn's tidy numbers: 99,984.26. So I guess it built up a bit of interest, just like Lily said.

I don't bother opening my purse. I just stuff the bill and the paper in my front pocket. A neon sign in the window of the credit union has caught my attention. It's a display that shows how much the Canadian dollar is worth compared to the American dollar, the Euro and the Japanese yen. Below that is the price of gold - $1,793 per ounce.

I start walking towards the waterfront and city hall, pushing that number hard into my memory so maybe I can figure out the value of those two gold bars later. Stupid. I can't remember how many ounces are in a pound but I can remember when Mackenzie King was prime minister of Canada.

I've got the envelope from the Paris lawyer in my hand because it won't fit in my purse. I presume it's Lily's will. There's quite a bit of paper or whatever in this envelope.

I stop at the light to wait. The sun is bright and the morning is already hot but it'll be cooler by the lake— I'm only a few blocks away. Looking ahead, I see him walking half a block ahead of me down the street, in no particular hurry.

The light hasn't changed yet but I'm already running across the street.

"Sam! SAM! SAM, WAIT!"

People are looking at me but I'm focusing on the back of that head, that guy walking up there, the one not turning at the sound of me shouting. I'm gaining on him, slipping between people on the sidewalk, nearly taking out an old lady with a cane. He turns right off Bernard onto Pandosy but I'm only a few seconds, maybe 10, behind.

"SAM! WAIT UP!"

I charge around the corner and there's no one there. It's a blank wall on my right until the alley halfway to the fountain at the end of the street. He couldn't have got there before I came around the corner, even if he ran, so I keep running, right into the alley to check.

Nothing.

I'm huffing and sweating.

I must be going crazy.

I bite my lip hard and turn back to the street, looking carefully up and down both sides, before heading towards the fountain. I try to keep my face frozen but it is melting as I keep walking, behind city hall to the Kasugai Japanese garden. The gate is open and my feet scratch onto the gravel path. There is a bench and no one is here. I sit on it, breathing fast and hard, but I don't cry, although I feel my face twisting all up because it wants to. I know that was Sam, I know it. I'm not seeing things. I'm not.

I finally catch my breath and the peace of the gardens takes over, the sound of the water, pushing away the noise of the traffic and the city. My hands are still shaking a little when I take my phone out to text Mom that I'm in the garden. While I wait for her to answer, I walk up onto the bridge overlooking the pond. The huge fat koi are gliding slowly, just under the surface.

The phone beeps. Text from Mom.

"Still in meeting. Can't meet for lunch til 1."

I look at the home screen on my phone. 10:32. I put my phone back into my purse and take out Lily's keys and then my keys, with the house key and Mom's extra car key, clenching them in my fist. I've got time to take Mom's car and go see what's inside that storage locker. The best part about Mom being in senior management is her reserved parking spot, in the shade along the north side of city hall.

I get the car running and put on some quiet pop station. My purse, the envelope and Lily's keys are in the passenger seat. My hands aren't shaking anymore but my head is pounding and my throat is sore. I reach under the seat and find a bottle of water. It's warm but I don't care.

"I'm tasting the poison, drinking the poison, the poison, the poison," the girl on the radio is cheerfully singing.

A little while after (Missy)

Sam is figuring it out. That's awesome.

He's feeling the hurt he wasn't feeling before but he's still got a long way to go. He's not chasing me away but he's been too quick to let me in sometimes. Like he thinks he just has to feel the pain I bring and endure it for a little while and that'll be enough. That's not the way it works but he'll figure that out, too.

I've seen all the misery there ever has been and it's all different and all the same.

I should talk to Cam about it but I'm going to wait until I have something to tell him. Some real news.

All that's really happened so far has been some good thinking, some really careful thinking about what he is and what he's supposed to do, instead of what he was doing before, when he was just doing stuff and then he hurt people, like he did to me. I think Sam wants to talk to someone about everything but he hasn't gone to do that yet.

Good idea because it's too soon for that.

He's not ready. He needs to think before he acts.

But if he's thinking about spreading his power around the universe and he's starting to take responsibility for what he's done, there's hope for him, and the rest of us, yet. And that's cool.

But all that could be chucked away real quick.

Here come Devi and Amara.

I have to decide right now whether I let them come or go stop them. I've never tried to stop anyone before so I don't know what to do and it would be those two against just me.

Why should I stop them? Why should Sam get the special treatment?

Because he is special, I guess.

Because guardians are coming to butt in on his personal suffering and that belongs to me.

I'm in charge here. I'm not the boss often but when anything is hurting, that's all me.

Sam hasn't done anything to show he realizes they're heading this way. If Sam doesn't realize they're coming, that's a great sign, and if he can feel them coming and he's ignoring them, that's a good sign, too.

I can do this. I will do this. He has to make up his own mind.

I go out to meet Devi and Amara.

I don't know what I'll say or what I'll do but I can't let them be with him. Not while I'm here.

I wonder if they'll try to hurt me.

They can try, I guess.

Letter Number Three (Lily)

To the family of David Willesden,
I am writing to you to explain what happened to

David and to tell you the truth about his murder. I am so sorry to tell you it was my mother who killed David. She did terrible things to his body and I saw her do it. I'm not telling you that to injure you further, but so that you'll believe me. I swear to you he died instantly and he was not frightened. He was so young and innocent but he saw us do some things he should not have seen. It was not his fault; he was just a curious lad. We killed him not out of anger but out of fear that he would not be able to forget what he saw, that he would have to tell someone such a big secret. Even today, I can't tell you what he saw. I can tell you my mother is now dead, herself murdered by people who hunted us around the world, for a very long time. That is no excuse for what happened but it does explain why.

David's death and the investigation into his murder were well-reported, so I will give you information that few people know. There were three major points of evidence that were never disclosed to the public.

A piece of David's shirt was never recovered from the scene but I include a small piece of it in this letter. The medical examiner's analysis will confirm it is his.

There were some articles of women's clothing found in the alley nearby, covered in David's blood—those were my mother's clothes. The most unusual item of attire would have been a large, custom-designed white brassiere with extensive underwiring for support.

Finally, to the frustration of the police's forensic experts, there were no fingerprints, hairs or even DNA found on the woman's clothes, David's clothes, or anywhere in all of the blood in the alley or the surrounding area that could identify the killers.

I write to you with only one intent: to beg for your

forgiveness. I am deserving of nothing but your hatred and your desire to see me punished for the crime I witnessed and did not prevent. I know that but I also know I must face what happened and the tragedy and suffering I brought into your lives.

Sincerely,
Lily
Kelowna, BC, CANADA

Bodie's fourth question (Sam)

What did you lose when you destroyed Lily's essence and made her human?

That wasn't about me, that was about Lily.

I lost someone strong enough to help me get through this but I gained because I made something Lily wanted more important than something I wanted. I put her wants ahead of my own.

I could still do that.

I can still do that.

She was already human, she just needed to complete the physical transformation. Having the power or not having the power wasn't important. It was about how she acted and how she took responsibility.

Maybe I could do that, too, if she was here to help me. I don't have Lily anymore. I didn't lose a thing but I thought I had lost everything when she became human and then when she died.

Now that I've lost her and lost everything she was, I know what I've lost. I know I'm lost, just going around in circles with these questions Bodie gave me.

But something's happening, something's changing in me. I can feel it.

Behind lock and key (Kathy)

I've never been to one of these self-storage locker places before but I get out of the car and act like I know where I'm going, walking past the office. There's a lady inside on the phone who doesn't seem to notice me while going through a stack of papers, so I head down the third row towards locker 358, the number on the key.

I have the place to myself.

The sun has already warmed up the pavement and the metallic doors are casting off lots of heat. I'm thirsty again and I didn't bring any more water with me.

I put the key into the lock and pop it off, dropping it into my purse before it burns my fingers. Luckily, the metal handle at the bottom of the door has some rubber covering on it so I won't burn my hands pulling up on it. I look down the aisle both ways but there's still no one here. I can hear the sounds of the highway and my breathing, which is fast and nervous.

The door comes up easy and quiet when I pull on the handle.

This is a small storage space—you might be able to fit a minivan inside but you wouldn't be able to open the doors to get out. There are eight identical big blue plastic containers inside, stacked neatly.

I shiver as the cool, musty air moves past me to mix with the heat outside. At least there's no hearse in here, like there was for Clarice in The Silence of the Lambs.

Quid pro quo, Lily. It's time you gave me some answers now.

No, wait, it's like those guys on that TV show when they auction off the storage spaces after the owners disappear and no one is around to pay the bill.

I wonder what they'd pay for this one.

I put my keys and purse down on the floor just inside the room and walk up to the first bin. The top of it is chest high to me, stacked on another below it. I grab the handle and pull the bin, which is lighter than I expect, towards me. After it is halfway off, I lower my end to the floor and some of whatever is inside shifts a little but I don't hear anything break. I stand alongside the titled bin and reaching around to the opposite handle, swing it out and carefully drop the other end onto the floor.

I pop the lid on one side and then step back.

Let's stop and review, class. Best friend has left you big pile of cash and big mystery about who she is, starting with a freaky letter where she says she's hundreds of years old and only just recently became human. Hmm, she didn't say *what* she was before that but that's a problem for another time. Let's go back to the real world.

There's a safety deposit box of hers downtown with two solid gold bars inside of it, there's whatever is in this storage room and there's whatever that lawyer in Paris has. What could be in these bins other than extra clothes or stuff her mom, or whoever Cindy was, owned? I force myself to stop thinking. Find out what's real and then maybe you can have some answers.

I pull the lid right off and lean it against the wall before looking inside the bin.

Lily's face is the first thing I see.

It's not her, exactly. She's got long, blonde hair here and her arms weren't as thick as what I can see here but the face is dead on: there's that distant look, a little bored, someone with too much on her brain or who knows too much. In the painting, she's topless and her arms are reaching behind her head to braid her hair. There are two women, servants maybe, with dark skin, one on each side but behind her, the one on the left is cradling a golden pot and the other one has a red and white jewelry box.

The canvas is not framed and the colour and depth of the oil on it shimmers, even here in the shade.

I'm not crazy about topless Lily, even if she's not looking at me, so I turn her over and lay the painting face down on the bin next to me. There's writing in the bottom corner. I bend to have a look.

"Pour Lilith, Chassériau" it says.

Never heard of him but I bet he's French, I chuckle to myself.

Inside the bin, there are some sketches on paper and canvas but the artist is not the same as the painting. Underneath those, there's a rolled up rug that looks like it's from the Middle East or maybe India. In the bottom, almost hidden by the rug, is a small square clay sculpture of some sort. I pick it up carefully with both hands.

It's a nude woman with big, round boobs. She's not exactly like Cindy but close enough. She's got wings and her feet are like an eagle's talons. She's standing on two lions and there are two owls, one on either side. She's got some sort of headdress on. The sculpture seems to be made of a beige clay.

"Okay," I say to no one but the clay woman. I put her back inside the bin, put the painting back on top but face down and close it, snapping the lid shut.

"Excuse me," A strict woman's voice says behind me.

I swear my head hits the ceiling from jumping so high. I turn around so fast that I almost lose my balance, my chest hurting because my heart wants to jump, too. My eyes squint to see the lady from the office, since the sun is behind her, bouncing off her bleached blonde hair that can probably be seen from outer space.

"I'm sorry, dear, if I frightened you," she says, her voice softer now as she steps inside so I can see her better. I shouldn't be scared since she might be five feet tall, even with her pumps. Her perfume finds my nose right away, sharp and thick.

She holds a clipboard out to me. "I just need you to sign in, if you could, and then show me some ID, please," she says, smiling and all business-like.

"Sure," I gasp, taking the clipboard. She holds a manicured and painted-nail finger pointed at a box on the piece of paper and I sign in it.

I get away from the perfume and grab my bag at the door, glad she came when I didn't have any of the bins open. She writes down my driver's license number and compares its signature to the one I put on her sheet.

"Okay, thank you," she says. "Next time you come, don't forget you have to sign in at the office. I guess you didn't see the sign."

"No, no, I missed it," I say, shrugging my shoulders and hoping she leaves, like five minutes ago. "Sorry about that."

"No problem. I'll leave you to your business. If you need help getting anything to your car, just come to the office and I'll get Marcel," she smiles and backs away.

"Thanks, and I will," I put on my happy face back. Yay, she's leaving.

"Enjoy the sun," she says and she's gone, her heels tapping on the pavement.

I blow out a long breath, forcing myself to relax. I thought she was going to bust me or something.

Okay, back to work. I don't have all day. I have to meet Mom for lunch.

One down, seven to go. That stuff in the first bin must

have been Cindy's. Never would have imagined her to be a lover of antiques or of paintings where Lily is topless. Although I can see her wanting a sculpture of herself with her boobs front and centre. That makes me giggle a little to myself and I relax. That'd be the day my Mom would ever want a painting of me with my boobs hanging out for everyone to see.

The next three bins are more of the same—sculptures, paintings, rugs, some fancy silk clothes with cool pictures on them. Some of the sculptures and sketches either remind me of Cindy or definitely look like her. The rest remind me of Lily, although I don't see anything else that looks like her as much as that first painting did.

The fifth bin has a big wooden sculpture of a raven in it and two big shiny wooden jewelry boxes. The boxes aren't identical but they look like they were made by the same person, all black and covered with this fancy silver and gold design on the lid. Inside both of them are rings, stones, necklaces, chains, pendants and earrings—carefully organized in little drawers. Mom's not a jewelry person, so neither am I, but all of it looks old and I think there are lots of diamonds and gold. I remember that the test for a pearl necklace is to gently scrape your teeth on it and it should feel gritty, not smooth.

"Uh, yeah, I'm not putting that in my mouth," I say to myself, tucking the necklace I had in my hand back into the drawer and closing it.

I close this bin and push it aside. I'm sure it's all worth a fortune but it doesn't tell me anything I need to know about Lily and where she came from and where Sam might be and what he knew about any of this, if he knew anything at all.

The sixth bin has nothing in it but beautiful quilts.

Too hot out to even look at blankets, even fancy ones with lots of embroidery. Grandma would be impressed with these, I'm sure.

The seventh bin has some strange looking musical instruments, mostly drums, in them.

Good thing I don't need to move the eighth bin because there's no way I could lift it without a lot of help, since it's so heavy. I crack off the lid quickly, expecting the same fancy and weird stuff I've been looking at for the last hour.

The one end is filled with books but the end closer to me has photo albums in them. I grab the first one and open it.

There are pictures of Cindy and Lily and they look just the same but their clothes and hairstyles are different from what I saw them wear here in Kelowna. I leaf through the album quickly but it's just shots of them alone or together or sometimes with other people I don't recognize. Okay, I recognize the Parliament buildings in Ottawa behind them in one shot near the back of the album.

Wait a sec.

One of Lily's letters about one of the people she apologized for she and Cindy killing went to Ottawa.

"The art teacher," I whisper to Lily and Cindy smiling at me.

That would explain the clothes and the hair. So was this photo taken in 1999?

But that's impossible. They look identical to how they looked when I knew them.

I put the album down and start quickly rifling through the pages of the other albums. The farther down I get in the bin, the older the albums get. The last two albums are super old but in good shape. The pictures are all in black and white but there they are, the same age as always. Near the back of the last one, there's a picture of the two of them standing in old formal dresses between a more serious man, with a sharp part in his hair, a full mustache and wearing a tidy suit. Behind and above them is a sign surrounded by lights.

I squint to read it.

"Westinghouse Electric and Manufacturing Co. Tesla Polyphase System."

Beside the photograph are two ticket stubs, one with the face of Abraham Lincoln on it and the other has George Washington. To the right of their pictures it says "World's Columbian Exposition Chicago. Admit The Bearer. 1st May to 30th Oct. 1893."

"Shit. Oh shit, oh shit, oh shit, oh shit." I hear myself saying because it's too big to keep in my head. I close the album and look away, staring at the dull metal walls, wanting to see something else, even the painting of top-less Lily, but the picture and those tickets are burned on my eyes.

I'm trying to breathe but the hot and dry air isn't moving into my lungs. There are spots in front of my eyes, even when I close them.

"Don't faint, don't faint, don't faint," I tell myself, biting my lip hard to shake myself out of this. Finally, after a minute, it passes and the spots go away and I feel like it's safe to open my eyes again. It's a good thing I was looking at these albums while sitting on one of the other bins or I would have already passed out. I swallow hard a couple of times and things clear up.

My cell phone beeps inside my purse at the front of the storage door and I squeak in fright, so scared and still so out of breath that I can't even scream.

It beeps again.

I put the photo album down and walk between the bins to the door. It's getting hotter. I grab the cell out of my purse and read the text from Mom.

"Where are you and where's my car? Starving for sushi. Pick me up."

It's 12:43. Shit, I've been here almost two hours and it feels like I was here for like 20 minutes.

"On my way," I text back.

I go put the photo albums away and close the bin before I notice I forgot to pick up that last album from where I left it on top of the other bin. I wiggle my way out and put the album down with my purse. I have to stack the bins up again or I won't be able to close the door. By the time I'm done, I'm puffing and sweating. I grab my purse and the album, step outside and reach up to close the door, swinging it down.

I take the lock out of my purse and slip it on quickly before running the whole way back to the car. The lady in the office must be on lunch because there's no one there now.

I crank the air conditioning on full blast cold once I've got the car running. My purse is sitting on top of the photo album on the passenger seat. I put both hands on the steering and take a deep breath. I can do this. When I pull into the parking lot, there's Mom coming out the door. I realize I have no idea how I got here. I don't remember a single thing from the last 15 minutes driving here because all I could see was Lily and Cathy in their Victorian style dresses with that man and knowing that picture was taken more than 120 years ago.

By the time Mom gets to the car, I'm hunched over the steering wheel, bawling my face off.

At this moment (Missy)

"Hi," I say to Devi and Amara. Maybe if I'm nice and respectful, this will go okay.

We're not really anywhere in particular but we're not too near Sam. I've taken physical shape because…well, I'm really not sure why, except that I like it and that's enough. I think because I also want them to see me properly. Okay, it's because I want Amara to see me and not like it. That's not nice but I think she's not very nice and she's a big reason all of this is happening so why should I be nice to her?

"Who are you that you think you have the right to block my progress?" Devi says, all bossy.

Both she and Amara are really pretty when they take their physical shapes. Amara is smart enough to be scared when she looks at me but Devi is not. I might have a problem with her.

"I'm not letting either of you guys go any further for now, okay? I want you both to wait until Sam is ready," I tell them with my best voice and smile, trying to be friendly.

Amara shivers when I talk. She doesn't know me that well but I spent a little time with her, but not too long, after Lily killed Samael so she knows who I am and what I do. She doesn't want to feel like that again because it hurts too much. Even being this close and looking at me bothers her. That's good.

Devi doesn't really know me but that's no big surprise. Why would she? Why would any of them? I'm called Missy but I know my real name is Misery. They know about me, maybe, but they don't really know me. None of them do until I show up and then they never forget me. I make them feel bad because they've lost something or done something wrong. That doesn't happen to guardians very often.

"Well, Missy," Devi says in a tone I don't like much, "I do not believe you understand what is transpiring or how important our business is with Sam. He has to take control of himself immediately. This situation is unacceptable to me and I will not tolerate it."

"Why?" I ask, still trying to be nice and because I don't understand what she's saying and want to know.

Devi looks at me like I just slapped her. Okay, this isn't going to go well at all.

"Why, you ask? Missy, you have no authority to question me and I fail to see how your present influence over Sam's emotional state has any bearing on the final outcome. I will ask you only once more to step aside." She's not mad but she sounds scary.

"I'm sorry this isn't what you want and I wish I could help you but I can't do that, Devi. Both of you have had lots of time already with Sam, so now it's my turn," I say, keeping my smile up but not as much as before.

Amara tries to stop Devi but she's not fast enough. Devi hits me with all of her power, going all around me and in me and through me. I always wondered how it might feel if another guardian tried to attack me.

Now I know.

And now Devi knows, too.

But that doesn't stop her from trying some more.

Amara has already run away but Devi is still here, still trying to find a way to get me. She has to stop soon or she'll hurt herself.

"Devi, stop. Stop, okay?" I tell her, holding her in place real soft. "You can't get past me."

She squirms and shakes and now she's really hurting

herself but she won't stop.

"I am in control, I am in control, I am in control!" she's yelling.

"No, you're not," I say, getting annoyed. "Who told you that you're in control?"

That stops her. She looks at me for the first time. She really sees me now and she's trying to understand.

"How are you stopping me? How is your power greater than mine?"

I let her go and step back.

"I don't know but I know you can't control me and the harder you try, the more you hurt yourself, and I don't want you to hurt yourself. Well, not too much," I say, proud of myself for standing up to her.

"But why? Why are you here with him? What stake do you have in this?" She is calm again, at least on the outside, but her voice has a higher pitch than before, like she's begging me for answers.

"I'm supposed to be here and he wants me here now, not like before when he wanted to hurt me and kill me even," I tell her, being honest even though I don't have to be and I could just tell her to go away. "And even when I'm done, there's someone else who probably gets him after that, and that's not you."

Oh, that was the wrong thing to say. Why did I have to mention Cam? Now she's really mad again.

"I will not simply stand aside while you and your ilk devote yourself to him. He is not even human anymore so he should be of no concern to you," she shouts, all huffy. "I demand you step aside or there will be serious consequences."

She's so serious that it makes me want to laugh at her. I hold in my giggle and pretend I'm like Cam and talk to her in my best calm and serious voice.

"You're right about him not being human anymore but he still acts and thinks like one and he's really hurting right now so I get to be with him," I say. I'm doing my best to be polite but I realize I'm starting to get mad a little. She's not listening to me. "And you can't threaten me so why don't you do what Amara did and turn around and go somewhere else? You had your turn."

She looks at me all panicky now.

"But that means…" she stops, covering her eyes with her hand.

I don't say anything. What's there to say? She thinks she's all about control and she thinks she can control Sam. Well, she did, until just now. Boy, what a shock that must be to her, to find out that she doesn't get to just boss around Sam when he's feeling like this and I'm around.

Finally, she drops her hand and looks at me. She lowers her head and talks nice.

"Please accept my sincerest apologies, Misery, for my rudeness to you."

"Aw, that's okay," I say back. "You didn't mean it."

"I most certainly did mean it and I am equally sorry for it now," she says, staring at me. "I have one critical task left and I should leave you to complete yours."

"Okay, Devi."

"Will you deliver a message to Sam for me?" she looks at me, hopefully.

"You know I can't do that," I say softly, shaking my head and looking down. I hope she doesn't get mad again because I'm glad she's talking to me like this now. "Even if he would listen to me and whatever message you'd give me, it wouldn't matter. Sam has to figure things out all on his own. That's the way I do things."

She doesn't say anything back and when I look up, she's already gone away.

Well, that went good. Nobody got hurt. I looked after Sam. Cam will be happy I stood up to them.

Yay for me. I'm so awesome.

I hope Sam remembers later what I did for him.

Letter number four (Lily)

Dear Mrs. Jamieson,

I am writing to you today to apologize and to take responsibility for the death of your husband, Gary, in 1999. He disappeared from the school parking lot around dinner time that day and I disappeared as a student from the school that day, as well.

Gary was a good man and I adored him as a teacher. He was able to reach me in a way no teacher had ever been able to before. He spoke to me in a way that made sense. I have had two mentors in my life and he was one of them. Both of my mentors are dead now and so is my mother, who killed Gary and dumped his body into Algonquin Park. He begged me to spare his life and I tried to stop her but I couldn't. I didn't want him to die. She was angry with him for the role he played in my life and she felt threatened by him, so she lured him out of the school and murdered him. I got there a few minutes too late. I didn't want to lose him and my mother, too, so I helped her take him away. I'm sorry for what she did and what I did afterwards. It was so wrong and I can never make it right.

If you direct the Ontario Provincial Police to the Whitney Lake access road off Highway 60, have them drive up the road for about 12 minutes. Gary's remains will be found about 200 metres north of the road. We did not bury him so almost all of the bones will be gone but the jaw bones will still be intact, along with some larger bone fragments from his femur, because cases I have read about show that human bones can remain outdoors for more than 50 years before finally breaking down I am not telling you this to be cruel but only to be precise, to help the police locate what is left of Gary.

He did not suffer. His death was sudden and instant.

I hope you and your children can finally and truly mourn Gary, giving him the proper burial he deserves. I am to blame and I deserve all of your anger. I beg for forgiveness but I expect none.

Lily
Kelowna, BC

Bodie's fifth question (Sam)

What is left of you, Sam, and what are you becoming?

This is the middle question, the central question, and the one where he said my name, so it must be the most important. The first four questions were all in the past tense and asked me to justify my mistakes, to make sure I understood the worst things I had done. This is the question that is about now and about where I'm going. It can't be answered without answering the first four questions and the last four questions can't be answered until this one is.

He wants me to address my name, my identity. Okay, I get that.

This is the "Who am I and who do I want to be?" question.

And there's a third question Bodie buried in there, a little joke that is completely serious, once you strip away all of the extra words.

"What is Sam?"

Sam-I-am.

Har, har, Bodie, never heard that one growing up.

But I get the real question, because it forces me to look further in the past than just my past, to think about what Amara made me from.

What is Samael?

That Sam I am, too, and that's not funny at all.

Amara saved that little piece of him because she loved him so much but how was that possible? Why didn't Crocodile notice it when Samael died? I wish that little girl would give me the name she gives other guardians but she insists I'm Alligator and she's Crocodile. Based on what we've done and what we can do, maybe those are good names for us.

Maybe Crocodile did notice Amara saved that little piece and didn't care. It was just a fragment, not enough to bring him back. Amara probably just thought she had some memento of him or something, until Bodie told her that she could actually do something with it.

But now that I think about it, I know the answer and Bodie knew it all along.

Samael had that dark piece in him but it wasn't really part of him at all, it was something extra, and I bet he really didn't know it was even there. And now it's in me.

Did he know it was there, separate from him? How could he have known that? But if it was something separate from him, how did it get there? Was it put there by someone or something? I couldn't see this possibility before but now that I'm trying, really trying, to figure out what I'm supposed to be, as a human Sam and what I am now and what I can do now, it's right in front of me, staring me in the face

But why don't I ask Samael myself? Why guess?

I can stay here with Missy but I can go back to Samael, just like I did to Bodie and the others that night at the pub, when Bodie asked me these questions. I can think about things and come to my own conclusions but Bodie would want me to do my homework and explore, not just sit here and mull over it.

I don't even have to think about it, really. I wonder about Samael and I'm in a dark place, not with Missy anymore, but in another place and another time. I'm still there with her, I can feel that, too.

How can I be in two places and two different times at once? That's a question for later.

"Who are you and what are you doing here?" Samael asks me.

He does not take a human form but I remember Lily telling me how he despised humans and wanted to exterminate us. He's all around me, here in the dark, and that has to be enough. I don't know when this is but it's not long after the beginning of everything.

"I'm Sam. I'm–" I stop myself because I can't tell him about Lily killing him. I don't want to mess anything up more by going back, like they do in the time travel movies, although I think I'm going to be screwing something up, just by doing this. "I have a question for you."

There is a short pause.

"Ask me then."

"Do you know about the darker piece of you that I also have?"

There is a long pause, so long that I wonder if he's going to answer. So I open myself up, so he can see and feel that darker side, that power.

Then he answers right away.

"I picked up this darkness because it is an aspect of me, nothing more. I still do not recognize you. I do not see how your possession of it as well is relevant to me."

"I have been made from that piece of you, to help you finish what you want," I tell him.

His answer is quick and certain.

"I want maximum entropy, a full and complete peace. You are not that so you are of no use to me."

"Well then what am I?" I shout back angrily.

The same cool voice answers me.

"I asked you that question already and you still have not provided me with a response I understand."

"I'm sorry, Samael," I tell him. "I'll leave you now."

"Do not return."

And I'm completely back with Missy.

I don't really understand entropy but I remember it from physics class, one of those definitions I had to memorize for an exam.

It has something to do with energy and the loss of it. Mr. Davis explained it as a wind-up watch that eventually stops running. It's dead but it's not really dead. It just needs an outside force to give it some more energy again but without a force to do that, it will always, eventually, run out of power.

I guess that explains what Samael was after. He wanted a place where nothing could move, nothing could act because all of the energy and life was gone, with only him there to make sure it stayed that way. No wonder he wanted me to leave and not come back. My arrival and our conversation ruined that concept for him. He knows it doesn't work, that it can't end like that, but he can't admit he's wrong.

But he recognized the piece of him, now in me, that might have helped him make better sense of it. He could have used it to kill off humanity but he was so full of himself that he ignored it, because it didn't lead him to that peace he really wanted.

How stupid could he be? He had the power right in his hands and he didn't use it because it couldn't be pure and perfect if it wasn't entirely part of him.

No wonder Lily was able to defeat him so easily. His want for that peace is literally all he was. He couldn't see anything else.

That could be me but exactly in the opposite direction if I'm not careful. I could become all of that power and have nothing left of me. That's why I have to think about Bodie's questions and answer them. I wanted peace and safety for Lily and my family and I wanted Amara to leave me alone. Just because I want it doesn't mean that's the way it is or the way it should be, even with the power I have.

So now I can really answer Bodie's question, about what's left of me, what's left of Lily's Sam, and what am I turning into.

I am Sam Gardner, 18 years old and soon to be 19. That's still left.

My parents are Art and Anna Gardner. I had a sister, Sara, but I killed her.

Pete is my oldest friend but we haven't talked much since high school.

Kathy is my best friend and maybe there could have been something more but there can't be now. I would still like that but I would put her at too much risk. If I didn't drive her crazy, literally, Amara or a random baseball would come along and that would be that. I would lose her sooner or later and that would hurt too much.

There.

That's what's left. I still care about my friends and my family. I still wish them to be happy and safe and now I know that the best way for that to happen might be without me there. It's not my fault this happened but it's not their fault, either, and they shouldn't have to carry the cost of it just because I do.

So what am I becoming then?

Bodie used to spout all this philosophy stuff about transition and evolving consciousness and growing awareness, so the question doesn't surprise me. He wants me to figure out where I'm headed, not to control it, like Devi would see it, but to take responsibility for it, or take ownership of it like Dad always would say. I can hear his sermon now. "Son, you need to take ownership of your life. Your successes are yours and your failures are yours. Own them. Don't blame others when it goes wrong but give yourself credit when it goes right."

That's what I'm becoming. I've stopped fighting this power in me and I'm trying to figure out a way that it becomes part of my life without taking all of Sam away. I have to take responsibility for the deaths I've caused but I also have to admit I have done some good, too. I gave Lily her humanity, the thing she always wanted. I should have tried harder to save Sara before killing her but if I hadn't stopped her, she would have killed everyone and destroyed everything. That's a fact.

I can't let the mistakes I've made run my life. I have to do everything I can so that the mistakes I'll make in the future won't be so bad and won't hurt so much. That's how I own them, Dad.

Dad's still talking to me, and now Mom, too, about

being a good guy and a decent guy in a world that's not always good or decent.

I listen to them now, much better than I did the first time, and it feels right.

Facing facts (Kathy)

Mom doesn't do emotional so good. She opens the driver's door, urges me out, gives me a quick hug (and I'm careful not to drip tears or snot on her Donna Karan blouse) and shoos me over to the passenger side.

By the time I've walked around and got in, mom's fingers are flying across her smartphone.

"Okay, I've cleared my afternoon," she finally says, putting down her phone and grabbing her seatbelt. "Let's get some sushi and then clear all of this up."

She puts the car into gear while I'm still finding my seatbelt.

"C'mon, what did you find?" she demands as we bolt into traffic.

My purse is in my lap and underneath it is the photo album I took from Lily's locker and the business envelope from the safety deposit box. As usual, I've stopped crying before mom tells me to stop but that doesn't take away the feelings. I've been thrown into the deep end of this huge thing Lily was a part of and Sam knew about and I was just going along, completely clueless. Now Lily's dead and Sam's gone and I have to make sense of it.

I pull in a deep breath. I can do this. Just be cool like Lily.

Mom won't want to hear about how much I miss Lily, how scared I am about what's happened to Sam, how alone I feel, how small I feel because it seems like my best friend was hundreds of years old, however that's possible. Maybe Mom can figure that out.

"Start from the beginning," Mom commands impatiently, not allowing me to organize everything flying around in my head. "What was in the safety deposit box and is there an account in your name there with 100 grand in it?"

Her business tone settles me down. There'll be lots of time for crying. Gotta focus on what's in front of me and think clearly. Forget Lily - Mom's the best for that.

"It has $50 less than that now because I took out money for our lunch," I answer, trying to smile.

Mom doesn't smile back.

"I wish you hadn't done that," she answers. "We don't know where that money came from or if it's clean. And how did you get into the safety deposit box?"

"What do you mean, Mom? I just gave them the key."

"You had to sign something, didn't you?" Her eyes are on the road and both hands are on the wheel. She's not speeding but she's moving quickly through the traffic. We're leaving downtown and heading to her favorite sushi place, a little spot on Pandosy out in the Mission.

"Sure, a card."

"And did they ask you for ID or anything? Okay, forget it, doesn't matter for now. What was in the box?"

"The envelope for the lawyer in Paris is right here with my purse and stuff but I didn't open it," I say, grabbing her smartphone, which she left next to the gear shift. "How many ounces are in a pound?"

"16," she answers, automatically. "Why?"

"Hang on," I say. I've typed in "LBMA" into her browser and I've got the London Bullion Market Association. "I'm just looking something up. I brought the envelope that was there that had her lawyer's name on it. There were other papers there that I didn't bring. They looked pretty old and they said treasury on them and they were from a whole bunch of other countries. And there were some old coins, in plastic cases."

"Okay, treasury bonds and a coin collection," she mumbles, pulling into a parking spot beside the sushi place. "What else?"

The LBMA Good Delivery gold bars are 400 ounces. What was the price I saw again? Right, $1,793 an ounce. Mom is already getting out of the car as I've switched over to the calculator on her phone.

"Mom, wait, I have to show you something," I say, holding up the phone so she can see.

"717,200," she reads from the screen. "What's that?"

"That's the value in Canadian dollars of the solid gold bar inside the safety deposit box. And there were two of them," I answer, watching her face. It's not the most important thing to tell her but she's a numbers person, so it's a good place to start.

Mom's eyes looking back at me would melt those gold bars. She's measuring me. Mom refuses to be played by anyone, ever. I just hand her phone back, which she snaps out of my hand, before leading me into the now mostly empty sushi place.

She's all business with the menu and the server. After we order, Mom stares at the envelope that I brought with me and put on the table but doesn't open it. She tucks it under her purse, her lips tight.

"We'll open it at home," she says.

"But it has the name of the lawyer on it," I protest.

"I don't care if it has the Queen of England's name on it," she answers. "Kathryn, Lily dropped you into a rather large pile of shit, don't you think? You can't just blindly follow her instructions. You have to protect your-self. We're not going to Paris until we know what her instructions are to her lawyer."

"We? We're going to Paris?" I answer but she already pressed a couple of buttons on her phone and now has it to her ear.

"Alex, it's Gwen. Call me as soon as you get this. It's personal and it's urgent."

Alex is Mom's lawyer who has also become her oc-casional boyfriend in the last year. Well, I don't really know what the deal is with them. He's stayed over a few times but when I asked Mom about it, she wrinkled her nose at the word "boyfriend" and said they were both too busy for that.

"Now where else did you go this morning, after you were done with the safety deposit box?" she says, putting the phone down on the table.

I don't answer right away because Mom's hot green tea and my peach bubble tea is here. I suck on the straw to get some of that icy coldness into me, to settle me.

"I didn't get a chance to tell you about the storage place she has at Kelowna Self-Storage, so I went there to see what was inside."

"And?" she says, blowing on her tea.

All I can see again is Lily and Cindy in their fancy Victorian dresses posing with that man at the Chicago World's Fair, which was like 120 years ago or something. But now I feel calm because Mom can help me carry all of this stuff Lily left me, as impossible as it is.

So I tell her, first about the photo albums and that last picture I saw and I offer to get the album out of the car and show her. She just brushes me off, so I rush into telling her about the part of the letter where she told me her age.

"And the other bins were just filled with art and stuff," I say as our sushi arrives.

I take another sip of my bubble tea. I can't believe how much better I feel telling someone else. I wish I was talking to Sam about it but I can't think about him right now. Concentrate on this stuff and on Mom.

"So you're telling me Lily told you she's hundreds of years or more old and now you have evidence that supports that?" she says, expertly plucking a piece of salmon sashimi with her chopsticks.

"There's the pictures in the photo album and I can show you the letter when we get home, and everything on the laptop. She's got addresses to banks and stuff all over the world."

Mom finishes chewing and swallows.

"I haven't asked you for anything yet because I want to believe you but I need to see it for myself," she says, concentrating on my face.

As I chew on my ball of rice and fish, I pull out the account statement out of my purse.

"There's what's in that bank account," I hand her the slip. "Believe me, Mom. I'll show you everything."

She studies it and hands it back to me.

"There has to be a rational explanation for all of this," she says, putting some ginger and wasabi on top of a rice ball. "And when I say rational, I mean an explanation that doesn't include a story about a girl who is hundreds of years old or more."

"That's why I want to go to Paris and see this lawyer," I say, trying to keep my voice low and not clench my teeth, just as Mom's cell phone beeps. That must be Alex.

Seeing is believing and the only rational explanation left is that Lily is what she said she was.

But how did Sam get pulled into this? How did he find out?

Unless…

No, that doesn't make sense. He has real parents. He had a sister. He couldn't be like Lily and Cindy. That wouldn't make sense at all, unless somehow Sam was one of those people who was looking to find them and kill them.

But Sara's dead and now Sam's disappeared. That can't be right. Did maybe Sara know something, too?

And how do Cindy and Lily die within a year of each other after living all those years? Too many things that look like accidents are happening all at once.

I should be crying again but I feel all cried out. All of the possibilities make me dizzy but those aren't the important things to worry about.

Just asking all of these questions means I could be somehow be next to disappear or get killed and now that Mom knows….

That could be what Sam did. Maybe he ran away to protect us, so that whoever is doing all of this would spend their time chasing him and not worry about the rest of us.

I look at Mom, so logical and careful, ending her phone call across the table. We're not going to Paris, Mom. It was a mistake to tell you anything. Nothing can happen to you or Jill. No way.

Mom has waved the waiter over and asked him to pack up our lunches because we have to leave right away. Alex is waiting for us, she tells me too confidently, as if a lawyer will somehow be able to figure this out.

But I can't disappear. Mom knows exactly where I'd be going. She knows about the bank account, the storage place, the laptop, the lawyer in Paris. I did the rational thing and asked for help and told my mom. Now I'm trapped.

"Kathryn, let's go. Kathryn!" Mom is waving me to my feet.

"Mom, we have to be careful," I tell her as I stand up. "Too many people have died by accident and now Sam is gone."

"What are you talking about?" she says, brushing me off. "Do you mean Lily and Sara and Cindy? You couldn't just create those accidents, especially Lily's, and no wrong doing was found in those car accidents, with Cindy and Sara. That's ridiculous."

She signs the credit card slip and I take our sushi, now in two little Styrofoam boxes, while holding my bubble tea in its clear plastic container in the other hand.

If you can live hundreds of years, maybe you can make physics work for you and do things that look like an accident to human eyes. Anything is possible.

I follow Mom out, her heels clicking sharply on the floor and then the sidewalk.

I'm stuck with her now but I'd rather have her with me than no one at all and if there's anyone who can get to the bottom of this, it's her. She won't quit until we have answers.

She can worry about the legal and the rational but I have to stay focused on what doesn't make sense and believe in Lily.

Maybe if I do that I'll be able to see any "accidents" coming at us.

Maybe I'll be able to find Sam.

I saw him this morning or I thought I did.

I have to keep watching for him, no matter how much that hurts.

Still more moves to make (Amara)

I thought I was finished and Sam was ready to fulfill his role but it seems there is still more to do.

If Missy is with him, he has stopped looking outward, looking for others to blame for his pain, taking his anger out on guardians, and then humans, and then everything else.

By turning his eye inward, he is blaming himself. Worse, he is trying to accept what he is and take complete control of his power.

I have only met Missy once before, shortly after Samael's death but I refused to let her take a grip on me when there was so much to do and I still had a purpose, a goal. When I asked Bodie what was the point of sorrow, all he said was: "Cameron."

I still have not met this guardian or even know how I could find him.

That does not matter.

While Sam finishes finding him, I will explore my options.

Sam still has his parents.

Sam still has friends.

Sam still has weakness I can exploit.

Impatience (Max)

It's excruciating to watch how long this is taking, not that I have much time to watch anything. I take my eyes off the machinery for more than a moment and the whole structure starts to shudder and complain. I can fix it but each time it's harder and more difficult and it takes much longer. Everything is brittle and fragile now, including me.

Still Sam hesitates.

He's not ready to find me yet but he's getting closer. He's at least facing in the right direction, now that Lily's out of the way.

I know he has to prepare himself, like I did before I took this role, but I can't believe I whined and moaned about it as much as he has. Still he's done well to get to this point. I'm confident he's the right one.

I suppose I have to be confident, now don't I? If he isn't the one, then it was all for nothing. Everything will collapse. Everything will stop. Only entropy will remain. Samael will get what he wanted, except that he won't actually live to see it. Nobody will live to see it.

I need Sam to fix this shit.

So get off your ass, kid.

The first reply (Geraldine Brenner)

My dear Lily,

Thanks for your letter about Jeffrey. I remember your grandmother Cynthia well because she distinctly asked me to call her Cynthia, even though Jeffrey and everyone else called her Cindy. As you can guess, we weren't exactly the best of chums.

Your letter startled me because I always presumed the two of them ran away together. My parents made the same presumption. Jeffrey had disappeared before without telling us, once on a two-week tour of Alberta and

Saskatchewan playing drums for a band that needed an emergency fill-in and another time for a week or so on some spiritual thing that involved kayaks and a trip up the North Coast.

We didn't even report Jeffrey's disappearance to police until he had been gone at least a month and once we told them there was a woman involved and she was gone, too, well they didn't get too excited about finding them. We always thought he would call when he was ready but his relationship with his parents had been strained since his days as a rebellious teenager, and our relationship, since I was five years younger with distinctly different interests and values, never truly developed.

As the months became years, I only thought of Jeffrey when I would visit my mother and father. They would talk about him as if he was going to call anytime. They missed him but they just hoped he was happy. I hoped he was happy, too.

My father died in 1992 and my mother died in 1997.

Jeffrey, as far as I'm concerned, died to me the day he disappeared in 1968. I have pictures of my parents in my home but I have not looked at a picture of him since I packed up my mother's belongings after her funeral. My children never knew their uncle and I've never talked to them about him, although they know from their grandparents I did have an older brother.

I appreciate you writing to me about Jeffrey and I'm sad to hear he has been dead all of these years. Mostly, I'm just relieved that my mother and father weren't alive to receive your letter. I went for a walk along the Stanley Park Seawall today and stopped near Siwash Rock. Instead of thinking of Jeffrey, all I could remember was the great memories I have of bicycling with my husband

and my children on the Seawall.

I will not be calling the police or the divers, as you said. There's really no point.

I worry more about you, Lily. What a horrible shock that must have been to read in your grandmother's diary and then learn it was true. If you were close to her and loved her as dearly as I loved my own grandparents when I was a young girl, that discovery must have been hard to take.

I hope you can find some peace and understanding about your grandmother in the same way I found peace and understanding long ago about Jeffrey.

Sincerely,
Geraldine Brenner
Vancouver, BC

Bodie's sixth question (Sam)

What do you want?
I want Lily to be alive.
That's all.
She deserved better.
I want nothing for myself.

The letter and the law (Kathy)

We argue the whole drive back downtown to Alex's office in the Pushor Mitchell building.

I get emotional, Mom gives me the logic and we get nowhere.

So I try to talk Mom's language.

"I know you want to tell him everything but until you see what's in the safety deposit box and what's in the storage place and look at the laptop for yourself, do you think you should just rely on me? What if I'm not seeing it right?"

I can't explain it but I don't want to tell Alex everything yet. It's not that I don't like him. He's way better than most of the guys Mom's dated since she gave Dad the boot 10 years ago. I just want to keep this to ourselves and try to figure it out the two of us together first, before pulling in other people. Mom isn't going for that, which is why I'm now trying to give her a good reason for agreeing with me. If I can make it her idea, she'll do it.

She finishes parking and then looks at me carefully.

"You said there has to be a rational explanation for this," I plead. "Why don't you look at it all first and then decide about going to Alex? You know he's going to ask to know everything."

Mom has her cell phone out and is texting. As usual, I can't tell what she's thinking by looking at her face or her body. She's way too closed for that. I wish I could keep my emotions under the surface like she and Jill can.

"I'm asking him to come over tonight," she says, putting the phone down and starting the car again. "We're taking everything out of the safety deposit box and everything we can out of that storage locker that might help us. I want to see everything and I want him to see everything. Then we'll decide what to do. Agreed?"

"Okay, Mom," I sigh in relief.

Sophie remembers me at the Credit Union and lets me into the vault area right away to get to the safety box. When I tell her I'll be taking everything, she disappears for a minute and comes back with an empty cardboard box.

"This should be strong enough to hold everything,"

she says.

I help her lift the safety deposit box onto the counter.

"I won't put you in the room since you're just empty-ing the box. I'll just go around the corner and you call me when you're ready," she says, leaving me alone in the vault.

I move the cardboard box close and make sure she's around the corner before flipping open the safety deposit box. I try not to grunt as I lift the gold bars and put them into the cardboard box as quick as I can. I'm still breath-ing a little hard by the time I finish throwing in all of the papers and coins on top. I close the lid of the cardboard box and call Sophie back in.

"That was fast," she smiles, closing up the safety de-posit box and putting it away.

I huff as I grab the cardboard box, putting my arms underneath the bottom to make sure it doesn't collapse, and start walking out.

"Oh, dear, let me help you," Sophie calls but I'm al-ready around the corner.

"I'll be okay, thanks," I gasp back. "My mom will help me."

Mom is standing at the counter, watching me strug-gle with the box. Sophie runs by to open the gate. Mom thanks her because I'm out of breath as I walk through, my arms shaking.

"You have a good weekend," Sophie calls as Mom holds the door open and then walks past me to open the little trunk of her car. I rest the box on the lip of the trunk. My back and arms are killing me.

Mom tries to move in on me, to grab the box herself but I push her off with my elbow, take a deep breath, ease it into the trunk and slam it closed.

"Okay, let's go," I say, walking to the door, trying to be all business-like.

Mom gets in the car, starts it and drives away. She doesn't say anything until we're almost at the storage place.

"Are you okay?" she finally asks.

"I am now," I smile. "This was too much to try to figure out for myself, all this stuff about Lily and all this stuff and her past. I know you'll help me make sense of it."

"I hope I can," she says, pulling into the parking lot. She turns the key off but doesn't move.

"Kathryn, I trust you and I'm glad you trust me," she says to the steering wheel. "I'm trying to keep an open mind and not judge Lily or you but you know her story doesn't make sense."

I pat her on the leg.

"See for yourself and then decide what you think. That's why we're here."

She smiles at me and then we both get out of the car.

I march right to the office this time and sign in, to avoid a repeat of this morning.

"Hi, I'm back and I remembered," I smile at the lady behind the counter.

"I see you brought a helper," she smiles back, acknowledging Mom. "Do you need me to call Marcel?"

"No, we'll be fine, thanks, we're just going to put a few things in the car," I reply, signing the box on the clipboard.

"It's a hot one, so take it easy," she says, taking the clipboard back.

"Okay, we will," I answer, already backing out of the office.

Outside, I ask Mom to get the car and then I guide her down the right row to Lily's locker.

By the time Mom has shut off the car, popped the trunk and walked around, I've already got the lock open and the door up.

"We can't get all of this in my car," she blurts.

"I know. We're just here for some things I need to show you and Alex," I say, already opening up that first bin.

When I hold up the painting of topless Lily, Mom's eyes get all huge and she steps forward to take it carefully from me.

"I know," I joke, turning back to the bin to show her some of the sketches but it's all the other stuff and the photo albums I really want to show her. "Not exactly how you want to remember Lily, eh?"

"I know this painting," Mom whispers and then I hear it rustle as she turns it over. "Right, now I remember, Chassériau." She even says it with the French accent, like she knows the guy.

"You've seen it before? Really?" I turn back to her, startled, the sketches in my hand.

"Honey, if this is the painting I think it is," she says, turning it back so that it's facing me again, "there's another copy of it hanging in the Louvre in Paris."

I just shake my head. The surprises and shocks are piling up so fast that I'm getting numb. A painting of Lily in the most famous art gallery in the world. Sounds about right.

"Mom, you haven't seen anything yet," I hold out the sketches to her.

She takes them from me and I notice her hand is shaking a little. She lays them out with the painting on one of the other bins while I go to the back of the locker and open up the bin with the photo albums.

I carry them four at a time and pile them into the trunk while Mom studies the sketches. I grab the oldest album out of the back seat and leave it next to Mom, so she can look at it now. I go through the other bins and grab a few more paintings and that sculpture with the big busty lady, laying them carefully on top of the other albums in the car. One of the paintings I found is another nude one of Lily, this time a full body of her. She's got much longer hair here and there's a huge snake wrapped around her. Gross. I hope she didn't actually pose for that one.

That'll rock Mom's world. That little car trunk is getting full fast.

"Is this the photo you were telling me about?" Mom asks. She's rifled through the photo album and is now pointing at the Chicago World's Fair photo that shocked me so bad.

"Yeah, that's it," I answer.

She holds up her smartphone to me and there's a photo of the same man on the screen.

"What?" I ask, taking the phone from her.

I scroll down to read the Wikipedia entry about some guy named Nikola Tesla and how he came up with the AC current for electricity.

"Cool," I say, handing the phone back to her.

Her hand is shaking hard as she reaches for it.

"Mom?" I say, pulling the phone back. I don't want her to drop it.

"Cool? That's all you have to say?" Mom says, her voice low and angry.

I've never seen her like this, trying to hold it in but not succeeding.

"How the fuck is this possible?" she says, looking at me but she's not really asking me to answer.

That's the first time in my life I've ever heard her say anything worse than damn but it comes from her mouth so easily, I think she must say it often at work and when me and Jill aren't there.

She points to some of the sketches I handed her. She's mad and her voice is high and loud.

"I don't know who the hell most of those artists are but there's two that say Chagall on them and I know his stuff sells for millions. I saw an exhibit of his just after he died in the 1980s, when I was in university. He's one of the legendary artists of the 20th century."

"I know, Mom, I know. It doesn't make sense," I say, trying to calm her down.

She jumps to her feet, scooping up the sketches roughly with the photo album. She stomps to the car and throws them through the open window into the back seat.

"This shit can't be real, it can't be real," she announces to the air, looking up at the sky and shaking her head.

I don't say anything because I know Mom will cool down in a minute. I close up the bins and stack them quickly, then pull down the door and locking it up. When I slam the trunk shut, it seems to snap her out of it. She glares at me, annoyed, and gets into the car, so I quickly jump into the passenger seat.

"As soon as we get home, I want you to give me that laptop," she snaps, turning the key and revving the car up loud.

"Okay, okay," I say softly.

"No, it's not okay," she snarls back, slamming the car into gear. "Not okay at all."

Well, this is going great, I think, staring out of the

side window.

Maybe I shouldn't have grabbed that other nude of Lily with the snake.

A little visit (Missy)

Now that I can start to leave Sam alone for little bits, I go see Cam.

He's happy to see me, of course, because that means he'll get to be with Sam soon, too, and that's good for everyone.

We meet at our usual spot by the lake and he's waiting for me, just like always, sitting on the bench. He gets up as I come running over.

I hug him even harder than usual and that makes him laugh.

"Oh, Missy, I'm happy to see you, too," he squeezes me back.

I let him go and try to keep my voice down, not that any humans could hear us anyway. It's really early so the sun isn't up yet and it's super quiet.

"I didn't know what was gonna happen when Amara and Devi came and I was scared and… and I still don't know how I did that, how I stopped her," I tell him. I wonder why whenever I'm in a human shape, I start waving around my arms when I talk? I can't help myself.

"Grief and sorrow cannot be controlled," he answers, sitting back down and laying his little white cane against the bench beside him.

"You look great, Cam," I blurt out because he does, his brown hair all tidy and his big old sunglasses and that nice brown jacket and the buttoned-up shirt and the blue jeans and the boots. "No, really, you look great. Well, I know you can't see what you look like but you always look nice as a human. And what kind of boots are those? I never noticed them before but I really like them."

He smiles in my direction.

"They are brick bullhide cowboy boots, Missy, and thank you for the compliments."

"So now what happens? I don't think I'll need to be around Sam too much more. He's figuring it out, I knew he could do it, he just had to get out of himself for a little while and it sure helped that Bodie gave him some help. That was nice of him. Do you think Sam will be able to come back here?"

"Yes, he will come back here but I do not believe it will be for too long. It will be to say goodbye."

I had been looking at the pretty lights on the bridge over the lake but now I turn back.

"What? Whadya mean? Why say goodbyes? Where's he going?"

Cameron pats the bench beside him. "Come sit with me, Missy, and let me explain."

I hop on the bench and lean close to him, putting my hand on his shoulder. He even smells nice, too.

"Missy, I suspect Sam has to either do what he was created to do or he has to leave this existence," he says, talking out to the lake and not looking at me.

"When you say leave, you mean go to Camille, right? And when you say do what he's supposed to do, you mean kill everybody and wreck everything, right?" I ask in my best quiet voice.

"Yes, that is what I mean," he says in his nice quiet voice, turning his face towards me. "The longer Sam avoids his choice, the more things seem to fall apart. I think Sam is finding a rationale for whatever he's going to

90

do next. When he comes to me, it will not just be to accept responsibility for what he has already done. He will also be looking for forgiveness for what he is about to do."

"But why?" I ask, upset and forgetting my quiet voice already. "Can't he do what he wants? How can he have all of this power but his only choice is either to kill himself or kill everyone else? That's not a choice at all. That doesn't seem very fair. Now I feel really bad for him."

"Your pity for him is well-placed, my old friend," he says, nodding. "No one entity should have to bear the responsibility for what he has to do but that is the way of things. His power does not give him freedom, Missy, I believe it binds him to a task only he is able to complete. He can forsake this responsibility if he chooses but he will only be passing it on to another."

"What do you mean?" I ask, sitting up straight and facing him. "How do you know all this?"

Cam is not looking at me anymore. He's facing the water and I can tell he's thinking really carefully and saying what he's thinking out loud to me.

"There is another force at play here, Missy, someone or something who has a stake in the outcome of what Sam does," he says, quietly. "It watches us and it waits."

I'm getting frustrated now and that's something that never happens when I talk to Cam.

"But how—?"

He cuts me off, turning to me. His voice is urgent.

"Camille informed me that she felt another presence, when she went to Lily at the moment she died. The poor girl was terrified because she couldn't see who or what it was but she definitely felt it. Did you have the same experience?"

I'm on my feet now.

"I didn't see anything, there was nobody else around, it was just—" I stop.

I only looked at Sam, when he came and saw us standing there with Lily. I didn't even look at her. I saw only him and I followed him when he left. Lily was dead. The only thing that had to do with me was Sam and how he was feeling. I followed him and didn't look back.

"I didn't look at Lily at all," I finally say, quietly, staring down at my feet. "So I guess this other thing maybe killed Lily?"

"Possibly but I don't think so," Cam shakes his head. "Camille said she felt this presence because she is being drawn to it. Whatever it is, it is dying."

I look back at Cam but don't say anything. He's facing the lake again, thinking really hard.

I hate when he does that. It's his nice way of saying I'm too stupid to figure out what's going on. Okay, so I've got to be smarter and actually think before I talk. I'm not used to that.

"Okay, so let's figure out why this thing would come out now, when Lily died," I ask, sitting back down by Cam and putting my thinking cap on. "It's not like she was even a guardian anymore."

"With Lily dead, Sam turns towards you and towards me, to drive him towards a decision and taking action," Cam says, his voice more sure. "It all comes back to Sam."

"And you mean he either does it or he'll like have to kill himself? Really? Boy, what a crappy choice. I'd hate that if I were him," I say, standing up again.

"He will not be happy with either outcome but he will come to understand there is no right decision, no pleasing everyone, no happy ending," he says, standing up, too.

"Well, I'm going back right away because he's really gonna need me some more, you know. He won't find you until he's made up his mind, right?"

"Just before, I believe that is correct, Missy," his arms are already open to me.

"I guess this is goodbye, then," I hug him hard again, pushing my face into his shoulder.

"We do not know that for certain, but it may be," he says, squeezing me, his hands across my back.

I'm still having a hard time believing Camille even saw or felt anything but I don't say anything. If Cam can keep his deep thoughts to himself, then so can I. We just stand there for a minute and don't say nothing.

I let go first.

"I miss you already," I tell him.

"Being with you has been one of my greatest pleasures throughout my existence," he smiles at me, squeezing my hand.

"Nobody but you is allowed to say that," I squeeze his hand back.

"I know," he lets go.

"Okay, bye bye," I turn away and I'm running back to Sam. He's gonna need me a little while longer and I'm going to be there for him. He's gonna need my help and I'm going to give it. He's a nice boy with a bad problem so I think that's the right thing to do.

The second reply (Mike Henderson)

Dear Detective Jenson,

Thank you for speaking to me on the phone regarding your investigation into the death of my daughter and I appreciate your interest in resolving this case.

Brenda and I are still very confused about the whole situation. The photo you sent to us of Lily is certainly the young girl who lived here and the photo of Cindy is definitely the woman who lived with her and they were the ones who disappeared at the same time Rachel was killed. Even if Brenda wasn't in such poor health and could travel, I wouldn't want to come to Canada to help you. When it all comes down to it, I don't really care about everything you were telling me about their ages and their missing identities and the rest of it. These two women are now dead but they died before they could be brought to justice for what they did to Rachel, so this does not give me closure or any of that nonsense I'm supposed to feel.

You asked me for a written victim impact statement so I hope this satisfies you but I don't care what you do with it. My beautiful daughter died nearly 40 years ago and if it wasn't for the picture of her in my living room, I probably would have forgotten what she looked like by now. My wife never stopping mourning her and she talks about her constantly now that she's finally dying herself, about how she's looking forward to being with her again soon.

I don't believe it will happen. I don't believe I'll see either Brenda or Rachel after I die because I can't believe in a God cruel enough to take my daughter from me the way she was taken away and to make my wife suffer for the rest of her life like she did and now to be dying of cancer.

I wish I would have got to the mail before Brenda saw Lily's letter. The way it was written made me sick and reopened so much hurt for Brenda and anger for me. Brenda reads it every day but I have to leave the room when I see her with it or I would rip it from her hands and burn it. I can't touch anything that was also touched by the woman who helped kill Rachel.

Good luck with your inquiries but please don't disturb us any further. The light of our lives went out on that day when Rachel was killed and knowing who was responsible or how it happened won't bring her back to us.

Sincerely,
Mike Henderson

Bodie's seventh question (Sam)

How far will you go to get it?

I think Bodie wanted me to take this question literally. If all I want is Lily to be alive, then what distance am I willing to go to get Lily back?

Because when I think of it like that, I realize how much this power really is, how huge it is, and how hopeless it was that I could ever control it. It's way too big and I'm way too small.

There isn't any place I can't be and there isn't any time I can't be at, either. I imagine myself walking down Bernard Avenue on a sunny, warm morning and there I am, even though I'm still here, too, with Missy, as far away from where I'm also walking as I could be. I can feel the heat of the sun behind me, I can see the light making the white sails sculpture at the end of the street, right at the shore of the lake, shine and I can smell the water, too. It smells like the promise of spring but it is also carrying that stink of dead fish and weeds rotting underneath.

And then I hear Kathy calling, shouting for me. I don't need to look back to know she really sees me because I'm really here, really walking in this place, not just thinking about it, and I'm scared to be here, because how am I here in Kelowna and still in this other place so far away? How can I be in two places at once? Dad watched this show on PBS once and I watched a bit of it with him, but he was getting annoyed with me because I was texting during it. The show was pretty boring but it was about quantum physics, like what Sheldon studies on The Big Bang Theory when he's not being such a goof, and how particles can be in two places at the same time.

I still don't get it. I'm here with Missy, in another galaxy, so far from Earth that telescopes can't see this place yet, but I'm here in Kelowna, too, now running for the corner and turning around Pandosy, into the shade. It's cool here and there's no one who can see me so I let myself stop being in Kelowna. I'm all back but not before I hear Kathy calling me again and she sounds so desperate and I want to go back to her. She needs me.

That hurts. That reminds me that there are people at home who must be looking for me. Mom and Dad lost Sara and now I've disappeared. But I don't have a choice.

Or do I?

I can be in all places and all times, too. I don't understand how that is possible but I can do it. I look back and see when Lily and I met on the sidewalk that first day of school, and I follow Lily backward, rewinding her time on Earth quickly, and I see it. I don't just see it, though, I feel it. I feel Lily kill that teacher and I see her and Cindy dump his body in the bush. I feel Cindy rip that kid apart in that alley and then Lily kills a little girl. That girl is so small and pretty and I feel the wind as her body falls from the roof and I hear that horrible sound it makes when she hits the pavement and how final it is. Lily is so cold. When she kills that guy in the park, (hey, I recognize that place—that's Stanley Park in Vancouver), she's so cruel to Cindy that I feel sorry for Cindy for the first time.

I follow Cindy forward from here, past when she

meets me to the night she holds me against the wall, when she thought she was going to kill me. I see it from her perspective. I can see why she doesn't like me and how upset she is about the effect I've had on Lily. She's angry but more angry at Lily and herself when she tries to kill me. And then that anger turns to fear when it doesn't work out like she planned.

But here's something I didn't know until now.

Lily went to see Bodie that night, to try to figure out what was going on. I knew that but I didn't know what Cindy did.

Cindy met with other guardians, ones who could maybe help them. Lily was sure I could be saved. Cindy was sure I couldn't.

She saw Devi first. I can hear them.

"You have uncovered Amara's little surprise and now you seek my help, Cindy? I am flattered," Devi tells her.

"You knew Samael was a lie, so are you still with us?" Cindy asks, impatiently. She doesn't want to stay still for long. She feels exposed.

"I apologize if I implied I was 'with you' in any way, Cindy. My brothers have picked a side in this conflict, as you know, and I have told them I oppose their decision. But that does not mean I will fight them if it comes to that," Devi explains, choosing her words carefully.

"You won't have to fight," Cindy answers, shaking her head. "If you stand with us, your brothers will back down and Lily and I will at least have a chance."

Devi nods slowly, considering Cindy's strategy.

"I will stand with Lily but I will not stand with you. You are too unpredictable, Cindy. Your very nature rejects the concept of control. You embrace the uncertainty, the variability of life," Devi finally says, using that cool voice of hers.

Cindy laughs.

"I knew you would say that. I don't ask for me, I ask for Lily, and it will please her to hear your answer, Devi."

"I would not be so sure of that if I were you," Devi quickly responds. "The two of you have no idea of the forces you face."

"So give me an idea then," Cindy smirks.

Now it's Devi's turn to smile.

"I think not. Amara has planned this endgame thoroughly and she is in control now. I see no escape for either of you."

Cindy nods but the smirk doesn't go away.

"You believe in yourself too much, Devi. There are always unseen variables, too many to account for. Guardians are not pieces on a board and neither are other living creatures, especially these humans. And if Sam is what I think he is, he will answer to only one other but it won't be Lily, or Amara or you."

"I agree," Devi nods. "He will answer to Death herself."

Cindy shakes her head now, her smirk cranked up.

"No, not her. Him."

Devi laughs but it is not a real laugh. It is controlled and exact. It starts and ends exactly when it should.

"Missy and her little blind friend have no role to play here. You are foolish to believe so."

Finally, Cindy's smirk dies down. She and Devi stare at each other for a long minute, like they might fight right there. Then Cindy nods once, a slight respectful bow.

"Thank you, Devi, for agreeing to stand with Lily."

"That is not a permanent offer," Devi shoots back, sharply.

"Nothing is permanent," Cindy replies.

Devi tries to respond but Cindy is already gone.

I follow Cindy to a county fair late at night.

She gets on a Ferris wheel with Crocodile, the adorable little girl that everyone calls Death. I need to accept that's what she is but it's hard. Even now, I just want to go across the fair and win her all of the toys and give them to her. I concentrate on what they're saying.

"You know I'm not allowed to help you, that's the rules," the little girl is annoyed that Cindy has even asked her for help. She crosses her arms and looks so cute.

"I'm not asking for your help, Camille, my dear," Cindy explains. "I'm asking you to not get involved."

"You mean, if they start hitting and hurting you and that other girl, I won't come get you when it's time for me to come and get you," the little girl asks, now curious.

"That's right," Cindy nods.

"Can I do that? Is that allowed?"

"I am the beginning of life and you are the end of it," Cindy smiles, patting the little girl's head. "We are the true powers and we can do what we want."

"I don't believe you," she says as the Ferris wheel reaches the top. There is nothing but darkness outside of the lights of the fair grounds. "If we break the rules, then nothing is right. You can't be Miss Cindy and I can't be me and I can't not be me and you can't not be you."

Cindy's smile is gone and she's nodding slowly, her lips curled in thought. The Ferris wheel is bringing them back down towards the ground.

"I like you, Miss Cindy, but I don't think I like your friend, that Lily girl, but I can do something to help, I think," the little girl breaks the silence and she looks up happily at Cindy.

"What's that?" Cindy says, still thinking carefully.

"I pretty promise that it won't hurt you, not at all, not for you or for that Lily girl. When I have to come get you, I'll come fast and you won't have to wait not one second. What about that, huh? That sounds good."

Cindy stops nodding. The Ferris wheel reaches the ground and the bar opens to let them out of their carriage. She gets out and helps the little girl (now I know her name is Camille) back to the ground.

"Isn't my idea a good one? I think that's a pretty good idea. I like it. I don't talk big like Devi or Lily but I can think big. Really big."

Cindy goes down on one knee in front of the little girl so they are at eye level. Cindy spits in her hand and then holds it out to the little girl.

"Okay, I got your promise. Now shake on it," Cindy says with a smile.

The little girl makes a quick spit into her right hand and shakes Cindy's hand enthusiastically, her face bright.

"That's a deal, Miss Cindy! That's a deal!" She lets go of Cindy's hand and then holds out just her little finger. "Okay, now pinky swear, too."

Cindy holds out her little finger and the two of them hook their pinkies together.

It doesn't seem like a great deal to me but Cindy is smiling so I guess she was happy with it.

I follow her as she leaves the fairgrounds.

She's at City Park now, in Kelowna really early in the morning, along the path by the lake, and there's Missy, who get's all excited and jumps off the bench when she sees Cindy and gives her a huge hug.

Something's wrong.

I can't hear them.I come closer and I concentrate

harder but I can't hear them.

They are talking seriously now, I can tell that from their faces, and then they both turn and start talking to the bench beside them and then the picture fades.

I start the scene over and over but it never changes. For some reason, I can't be here.

Right.

The guardian Lily told me I can't find yet, the one that has to choose to come to me. I'm obviously getting closer but I still can't reach him.

Maybe I could use my power and rip this moment apart and pull him out of it? Not maybe. I could. But what purpose would that serve? And haven't I used my power enough just because I can, especially when I don't know what will happen when I do? I remember that I answered the last question by saying I don't want anything for myself and that's still true. Maybe there's a perfectly good reason for not seeing this other guardian yet, a perfectly good reason why he hasn't shown himself to me. I haven't figured out what that is yet.

I'm not in any danger and neither is anyone else that I can tell from this guardian so I leave Missy by the lake and follow Cindy, but there's long moments of black, when she's obviously with this other guardian, so I push to the end, where I'm alone with Lily and we experience each other's essences for the first time completely and there's Cindy alone, facing the other guardians. Kyle and Dan and Cherry and Ruby are hurting her. Camille doesn't keep her promise as much as I would have liked. I guess that's what a guardian calls quick. It looks to me like Cindy still suffers a lot before the end but Cindy doesn't seem to mind when she sees Camille coming towards to her. In fact, she smiles at her and reaches for her hand.

I'm not just watching. As Amara and Crocodile (I know now her name is Camille but it seems wrong to call her anything by Crocodile) come up to Cindy, I realize I could stop them.

I could change this if I wanted.

But I don't. I keep my power inside and I watch.

I'm going backwards again, to the other time Cindy was hurt by guardians and I see Lily take Samael and kill him, right in front of Amara, and now I feel sorry for Amara for the first time, too. This is where it all started. This is the moment I would change. It would be so easy.

Right here.

I could stop Lily from tricking Samael. I could stop Amara and her friends from hurting Cindy.

I could stop Lily from being so cruel, destroying Samael right in Amara's face. Except she didn't destroy that one extra piece of Samael. It seems she didn't even realize it was there but Amara sees it right away and takes it, saving it for later, saving it for me.

Lily was so terrible. I see her, all of her now, and I understand for the first time the guilt she was carrying. To become human meant to finally face what she had done, to Samael first, then to Amara and then to those people. There she is, the girl I love, and we're walking down the street at night towards the lake after our first date and she's putting my heart back in my chest and she's lying with me on the sand after saving me from Amara and we're lying in a bed with our clothes off and I'm in all of those times, all at the same time. I'm not in two or three or five or ten places or times, I'm everywhere and everywhen.

But it's deeper than that.

Even as I'm with Lily in all of those times, I'm still

going much further backwards with Lily and Cindy. They're always together, before there are humans, before even Earth is a real place, and then, for a single instant, right at the flash between nothing and everything (take that, Sheldon, there's the *real* Big Bang), Lily is alone, before she and Cindy are together.

I finally give in to my power to freeze this moment right here, right now, and I surround her essence in this void. I want so bad to be by her side.

But she doesn't know me. I could reveal myself to her now and she wouldn't know who I was. She doesn't even know who she is yet.

She not in human form but her essence stirs, as if she's heard something, and I realize she's sensing me, feeling my want. Her first conscious act is an awareness of me and my desire for her.

That's enough.

I release time and it rolls forward with an incredible release of energy and Cindy is with her, completing her.

I'm so close to her and so far away.

To answer your question, Bodie, I don't have to go anywhere.

I'm already there.

I'm already here.

Blood on the table (Kathy)

Mom is back to her scary calm self by the time we get home.

As we carry everything inside, I ask her what would happen if the cops came back with a warrant or something, like on the TV shows, and caught us with all of this stuff.

"I think they would have already done that if they had something," she answers with a shrug, not really convincing herself or me.

We carefully lay the paintings and sketches out on the dining room table and put the rest of the stuff on a couple of the chairs. I put the box with the gold bars and the papers from the credit union on the kitchen counter. Mom is examining one of the gold bars by the time I come back with Lily's laptop.

"What kind of person keeps gold like this?" she asks, putting it back in the box and putting the cover back on. "Nobody keeps gold anymore."

"Didn't rich people keep gold around a long time ago, just in case?" I say back, handing her the laptop.

She just smirks at me and nods, heading into the living room.

Jill gets home a few minutes later from school and I follow her into the kitchen.

"Hey, what's going on?" she asks, opening the fridge and pulling out the juice jug.

"Nothing," I say, getting glasses out of the cupboard for both of us. "Me and Mom are going through some of Lily's stuff and deciding what to do with it."

"The stuff the cops didn't take?" she says, pouring into the glasses. "I thought they took everything."

Shit, she's fast. She's just like mom. Even when she doesn't care, the bullshit meter is on and running.

"Uh, yeah, that's right, but they said we could have some of it back, so me and Mom went to pick it up," I answer, trying to be nonchalant and hiding my mouth behind the glass of juice.

I take a big sip to stop talking. Don't say anything more than that.

Jill puts the juice back into the fridge and walks past me, ending the conversation and her interest. She could care less about the stack of stuff in the dining room and the box sitting there.

Mom is on the couch with Lily's laptop, studying the screen carefully.

"Hi, honey," Mom says, not even lifting her head.

"Hey, mom," Jill answers without stopping, heading to the stairs. She doesn't ask why Mom is home on a work day. A few seconds later, she turns the TV on downstairs.

I need something to do so I empty the dishwasher and then start on dinner, going slow so we're not eating in the middle of the afternoon, like what happens when we visit Grandma's place. She gets so worried about people going hungry that as soon as lunch is over and the dishes are done, she starts with dinner. It's 4 in the afternoon and she's calling everyone back to the table. I can see myself doing that someday.

"I'm gonna text Alex and invite him for supper," I tell Mom, picking up her cell on the coffee table.

"Good idea, pumpkin," she answers, her eyes not leaving the laptop screen.

"Last client—I'll get dessert—there in 1 hr," he texts back.

I smile and put the phone back down. Somebody is curious and has cleared his schedule. I've gotten to know Alex a bit since he and Mom have been together. He's a good fit for Mom—just as logical and careful and focused as she is but in an easier, more relaxed way. He's eight years older than mom so maybe that's it.

Working in the kitchen, pulling lettuce and some vegetables out for a salad, helps me relax and think clearly, just like Alex.

We have to go to Paris, that's a fact. But I know what Mom's going to say. Why? Why do we have to go to Paris? Why do we have to figure out the Lily mystery ourselves? If it's as big as it seems, why can't we turn it over to the cops and walk away?

I wish Sam was here. He would know what to say, as usual. He knows how to convince parents and other adults of things they normally wouldn't agree to, either because he would get them to change their minds or because they would just trust him to make sure it turned out fine. He said once I was way better at it than him, but I could never do it with Mom. Not that Sam's parents aren't tough, but Mom's a single parent, so she's way harder to crack.

I keep telling myself that if I figure out the Lily mystery, I'll find out where Sam is, but do I really believe that? Have I been using that as an excuse to fight Mom on this? The deeper I get, the more unsure I am. I hope Alex can help. I trust his opinion and how he—

"Ahhh! Shit!" I shout.

I'm bleeding all over the cutting board. I've decided to add the tip of my finger to the carrots and celery.

I turn to the sink and start running cold water over my finger. The cold makes my finger go numb right away and I see the gash in my finger. Mom keeps her knives sharp, so it's a deep one.

She puts her arm around my shoulders, startling me for how fast she got here from the living room, and she bends to look.

"Oh, that's nasty, Kathryn," she announces. "Keep it under the water for another minute and I'll get the first aid kit."

She hustles out of the room and I can hear her jogging up the stairs to her ensuite bathroom.

I shake my head at how stupid I am. I can't carry all of this by myself. I have to trust Mom and I have to trust Alex. I have to let them help me and if that help means I have to let go of Lily and even let go of Sam, then I have to do that.

"You're right, Mom," I tell her after she comes back and dries my finger before tightly wrapping it with one of those new fancy clear bandages.

"No, pumpkin," she answers, patting my hand on the counter and looking at me. "You're right to care for Lily, no matter how it looks and how none of this makes any sense. She asked you to do this and you have to be faithful to your friend as best you can."

"Alex will know what to do," I nod back, putting my other hand over her hand on mine.

She smiles back, a much broader and fuller smile than I'm used to from Mom. She's happy that I like Alex as much as I do and it really bothers her how much Jill keeps him away.

"I think so, too," Mom says. "We have to be careful and he'll be able to tell us how to do that."

"So what did you think after looking at her stuff on her laptop?" I ask her.

Now her face gets dark and the smile goes away. She looks older.

"I think we might have to go to Paris," she finally says.

Talking normal, acting weird (Missy)

So when I get back, Sam wants to talk to me.

"Who were you talking to?" he asks me, trying to be friendly.

"My best friend," I tell him back.

"Why can't I see him?" he asks, looking confused. He looks pretty cute that way.

"Because you're not ready to see him yet, I guess," I shrug my shoulders.

He looks away and nods.

"Will you go there with me?" he finally asks. "I'd like to sit there with you and talk."

"Where? The lake? That's my special place with him," I'm already shaking my head. "I don't want to go there with you."

"Will you do it for me?" he pleads, his eyes wide.

"Why?" My hands are on my hips because I thought I made myself pretty clear.

He looks down at his feet and his jaw gets tight and his mouth curls up. He's about to cry but he holds it in.

"I have...to go...there," he says, looking back up to me and speaking carefully.

"You can go wherever and whenever you want from what I can see," I tell him, sounding all bossy, making things tough for him. He doesn't get any free passes to Cam. Nobody does. "Whatdya need me for?"

He takes a deep breath and I wonder if he's about to just kill me and get this all over with. But he doesn't seem mad or frustrated. He wants me to understand him, so if I don't want to go he won't go, but he really wants to go and really wants me to go with him.

He releases his breath.

"I need to go see Sara and I need you to be there with me, Missy," he says, real calm and quiet. "Please."

I come up to him and take his hand.

"When you ask me all nice like that, you know I can't say no," I smile and then we're standing by the bench.

It's the same time it was when I was just here with Cam, all early and bright in the sky. He's not here and there's no humans around, either, but everything and everyone is starting to wake up. There are a few cars on the street but they are far away.

"Will you stay with me?" he says, looking at me but still holding my hand. He's scared.

"Sure, Sam," I smile at him.

The instant he lets go, Sara comes out of nowhere and tackles him really hard, slamming him into the bricks on the path.

And then she's kicking him in the face, the kidneys, the groins, where it really hurts. Then she pries up a loose brick from the edge of the path, kneels sideways across his body, one leg across his chest, the other across his neck and pins his arms back so he can't bring up his hands to defend himself. Then she starts smashing the brick into his face and the side of his head.

She doesn't make a sound as she's doing it, so the only noise is the yucky sound of that brick hitting his skin and bones. It makes me shiver but I'm not cold.

Sam isn't making any noise, either, except for an occasional grunt of pain. He's taking every hit and he's not even trying to protect himself.

Finally, she stops and throws the brick away, its one side all red with Sam's blood.

She stands up and unbuttons her shirt, but instead of skin, it's the darkest black and it goes on forever and it's moving around lots like the waves on the lakes when it's all stormy.

Sara pulls her brother to his feet.

"This will make things right," she says.

Wait a second...

I take a step forward and then stop, because I don't know what to do. Cam told me that Sam might just kill himself somehow, turn himself over to Camille instead of doing what Amara made him to do and kill everybody else. Is he killing himself by bringing Sara back and getting her to do it?

Oh no.

Sam breaks apart in pieces and the pieces all fall into that black in a few seconds. She closes her eyes and sighs when it's all done. While Sara buttons up her shirt, Camille shows up and starts dancing in circles around Sara. Amara is here, too, and she smiles and nods at Sara in approval. Devi is with Amara but she stands to the side and doesn't say or do anything.

Sara stops on the third button and her hands don't move. Then she unbuttons her shirt again.

She turns and looks my way, seeing me for the first time.

"I'm supposed to get rid of the bad people in the world and the bad people like you everywhere else," Sara tells me.

Then Amara looks at me. The little girl stops dancing and looks at me. Devi is staring, too.

Oh oh.

The third reply (Paul Willesden)

My counsellor says I need to write some bollocks journal to "better organize my thoughts and direct my anger" and some other shite while the police investigate that letter I got about David's death from that bag in Canada. He's fucking thick as shit in the neck of a bottle but I'll do what the wanker says.

I don't know how this troll came to find out all that two-bob bit about David and the crime scene and how she got hold of that piece of his shirt but I still say she's a filthy liar. There's no way a couple of birds took out David like that, chopping him up like ground meat from the butcher. You can say it was you all you want, little miss, but I know for a fact it was Joey McPherson's men, sending a message to chief baghead to pay for my shit or it would be me mum next and they'd do that one more private, so they could really rough her up before killing her and then they'd dump her body in my bed, just like they did with the horse's head in The Godfather because those retards think they're the Corleones or something, and then they'd ring me up and say "That's too bad about yer mum, innit?"

I didna need to see the alley or read no police report since it was all over the papers. "Slash and Dash" was on the front page of the Sun with a picture of the Scotland Yard wankers in their yellow hazmat suits and blood all over the walls and floor of the alley. The Evening Standard had a different photo of some guy carrying out parts of David in a bag underneath the big black words "Clerk chopped up for day's receipts." In the days after, the papers wondered if David was linked to the racket, if the owner of the record shop was linked to the racket and then they wondered if he was a case of the mistaken identity and they were after some other stupid wanker.

That would be me, ya daft twats.

I was already rattling from the shakes but before I got really sick, I robbed five stores that night and West End places, too, but I didna hurt no one and I got every pound for Joey. I gave it to him personally and he laughed at me and offered me a spoon and a needle and I wanted it so bad but I said "Thanks, Joey, you're a good man, but I'm cutting back."

Can you believe I said "cutting back" after what happened to David?

Joey just laughed his fool head off and so did the rest of the huge lads he kept around him and said he'd see me soon.

But he never saw me again.

I thought of going to see him in the prison when they finally locked up that wanker two years ago but I thought there's no way he remembers some messed up junkie from the neighborhood. Just another twat-faced customer, one of many.

I paid my tab and I called my cousin Laura and she met me at the hospital and I went through my withdrawals with no methadone or any shit. I hallucinated about all the ways I had killed my baby brother and it would have put Tarrantino and those Hostel movies to shame. But I did kill my baby brother, by not paying for my shit, even after Joey's boys warned me lots of time, and roughed me up a few times, so they gave it to David, what they should have done to me instead.

I could barely even stand and I know I made a total bollocks of myself but I was sober at David's funeral and I've been sober since and I moved to Liverpool with my uncle Paul, the one mum named me after, and he got me a job and I've never been back to the neighborhood except to visit mum in her shithole flat that she won't leave because of all of the memories of Dad and David hanging everywhere. I stay there as long as I can manage, eat her wretched boiled potatoes and cabbage, leave her a few pounds and piss off smartly.

I don't recall no Canadian birds around Joey or his

boys then but I'm sure they had lots of birds they was banging, since they had so many pictures of the Queen in their pockets and paid for all the drinks in the clubs. They might have brought this Lily bird along to see what they did to David, just to show how tough they were and not men to be messed with.

I bet she couldn't get to Heathrow and out of here fast enough, back home to her snow and igloos.

Probably took her this long to get over the nightmares, poor stupid bird but I know she's still scared and talking out her arse that her sister did it.

But now she's just transferred them nightmares back to me and I ain't never been tempted to use again until now. But I won't because of you, David.

I'm a maggot who should feel like this every day for the rest of my life for what they did to you. You died like a animal and it wasn't right. Staying clean and visiting mum was what you did so that's what I'm doing. I don't know how to do anything else.

Bodie's eighth question (Sam)

Are you willing to always be near her but never be close to her?

I know what this question means. I realize that after being near Lily at the very beginning, before the universe even did its Big Bang, and there she was, before anything or anyone else. I could spend the rest of the billions of years with her, all at once, and share all of her experiences with Cindy and her learning about everything but she would never know I was there.

Even if I did reveal myself to her, she wouldn't know who I was and there's no guarantee she would even have feelings for me. She fell in love with the human Sam, at that exact point in her long life. Who's to say she would love me if she met me 30 years earlier or 300 years or 300 million years?

But then what was it she loved about me? Was it Sam? Was it the part that Amara put in me from Samael that makes me all dangerous? Or is it the combination of the two? Or was it also that she was ready to love and I was just in the right place? Probably some combination of it all that can't be copied again.

I'm overanalyzing this because this all goes back to earlier questions and earlier answers. Just because I would have the power to show myself to her, would it be the right thing to do? How would it change things? If I stopped her from killing Samael, how would the history be different? I know the history of me doing stuff with my power because I wanted to do the right thing has not worked out very well so far, with all of these consequences I didn't want and didn't see before I did them. That's not a good history and I have no reason to think this would be any different.

As usual, I have to take Bodie at face value when he asks a question. The important part of this question is not the last part, about being near Lily and never being close. It's the first part I have to focus on.

Am I willing?

Will I act on this or accept it and resist the temptation to change it?

I'd be changing it because it's what I want and I'd be putting myself and my wants before anyone and everything, with no idea if that's what Lily herself would want. How can I do that again?

I can't.

I will accept this because I have to. Stop talking. Stop thinking and accept these moments with her, close but unseen, as gifts. Amara didn't get to have that with Samael, Lily didn't get to have that with Cindy, no human who ever lost anyone has been able to go back and be that close with someone again. Why should I get more than the incredible gift I've already been given?

But now there's a different problem and I have to wake up.

While I'm here, I went with Missy to the lake, and Amara and Devi are there, and Sara is beating me and killing me and taking my power, all the stuff she wanted to do that night but I didn't let her. She's looking at Missy now.

Sara doesn't belong there. That's the Sara from the night we fought and I had to kill her. I needed to go through that again but this time to lose to her, to feel what it would have been like and it didn't feel like anything. It was stupid of me. I was testing this, testing the limits of my power, seeing if I could not only move myself through time but move other people as well.

I can but so what? And why can't I move forward, past this moment? Why can't I race to the end and see what happens? Is there something or someone in the way? And even if I could go to the end, would I? Would that be the right thing to do? Maybe I can't go forward because there are too many options.

Like the options here.

Missy can't get away and Sara already has her.

If I step in, I have to do it now. I can't wait or I'll be forced to go back and rewrite this moment and I don't want to do that because if I do that, I'll be tempted to rewrite all of the moments, where everything went wrong. I liked to think I was a good writer but it was all selfish, to make myself feel better and more important. That's what this would be, rewriting everything to my satisfaction. That's no life, that's fantasy. And I would know it was fake and perfect.

I'm back in the park in the night with Sara and I murder her over and over again, to make sure I really understand what I did but also to find other ways I could have taken but I don't see any. I get to be in all places and all times at once but I don't get to see the options, the different timelines and spaces, just like I don't get to go forward.

That's why I have to be willing to accept this. If I would intervene at earlier points and stop things from happening, I would be trapped in that moment. I would not be able to go forward because there would be no forward like there was before. My action would erase it.

So I kill Sara again and again and I know this is what I have to live with. I get to be close to Lily but I get to relive this endlessly, too, all the good and all the bad, melding together, but the good seems so small and so short and temporary. Those horrible moments, killing guardians, killing Sara, trying to kill Lily, are so much bigger and brighter. They hurt my eyes.

That's what I have to carry and live with, not just my power, but what I've done with it.

And now I have to use it again.

Carefully.

Protectively.

Like Superman. Strong enough to take over the world and make everything right but strong enough to hold it in and only stop what needs stopping. And then stop there.

I'm with Missy and it's as far forward in the now as I can go. Missy is trying to get away but there's no way she could get far with Sara after her. Sara has hurt her bad already, holding her like that. This is not a quick thing because Sara's got a cruel streak and she doesn't just want to get rid of bad guardians (or what she thinks are bad guardians), she wants to hurt them first.

Missy sees me and smiles.

"Cam," she breathes. "I knew you'd come save me, Cam, I just knew."

She's looking right at me but she's seeing someone or something else. I don't let that distract me.

"It's okay, Missy, I'm here," I tell her, putting my arm around her shoulder. She's shaking badly. "It's okay. I'm here like you were for me."

She nestles into my chest and sighs.

"I'm ready for whatever, Cam. Just tell him to do it."

"No, no, Missy," I answer, stroking her hair. "That's not the way this is going to be. I still need you. I still need your help but I also need to help you."

I hold on to Missy and look first at Amara and Devi. They must see something else and not me either, because they're looking at me as if they don't know me. Amara is biting her lip and shaking her head slowly in frustration. Devi has the most gorgeous smile, not her manipulative, conquering grin, but something more genuine. I want to talk to them and ask them things but I ignore them for now. There will be a lot of time to talk to them later.

The Sara I brought forward, from the night in the park until now, is frozen in place where I left her. Part of me leaves Missy's side and takes Sara by the hand, back to the park, back to the moment she can only have, waiting to attack me. As I leave her, she's already running and I feel her slam into me, the me back then and there, and the moment starts again, leading up to when I kill her.

That's enough.

I close off all time and places where I am, where I could be, and concentrate on the last forward moment, the only place I should be. I even stop being on the other side of the universe, where I've been sitting and thinking about all of this. All of me is right here in Kelowna now, on the shore path of City Park, early in the morning by the looks of it, here with Missy. I lead her to a bench and we sit together. She slumps against me, still shaking.

"She hurt me, Cam, she really hurt me. She really hurt me. It's like she turned me against myself. It was horrible and I couldn't do a thing to stop it. The harder I tried, the worse it got."

"Ssshh, sshhh," I stroke her hair again and squeeze her with the other arm, trying to get her to calm down . She's so upset that she's saying my name wrong or maybe I just thought I heard Cam and she really did say Sam. "You're okay now, Missy."

Missy starts crying but she doesn't have my full attention again. Amara and Devi are gone but now Crocodile's walking up the path towards us, her shoes clattering on the bricks.

"Hey, Alligator," she grins, stopping in front of me.

"Hi, Crocodile," I answer, smiling in spite of myself. She's just so adorable.

"Can I call you Camille, your real name?" I ask her gently.

She tilts her head, cute and thoughtful.

"You can but you may not," she scolds. "Camille is just one of my names and it's the name Mr. Bodie and Miss Cindy got to call me and you're not Mr. Bodie or Miss Cindy, that's for sure."

She points a finger at me, her face serious, her eyes

sharp.

"You call me Crocodile and that's it."

"Okay, okay," I laugh. "I didn't mean to offend you... Crocodile."

She relaxes and she's smiling again.

"I'm not here for anything," she says, shrugging her shoulders. "I just wanted to say hi and tell you how nice you look today. You haven't looked this nice since the day I met you, when I brought you those flowers and you went away to try and find Lily."

When Cindy died and Lily was fading away and I used my power, but I really didn't know what I was doing, to try and find Lily and bring her back. Crocodile had brought flowers. When Lily came back, she loved those flowers but they sure scared the shit out of Bodie. He wasn't expecting that.

"Thanks," I answer back. "I had almost forgotten that."

She just smiles and nods.

"I know. But now you won't forget, right, how we met and what you did?"

I nod back, my smile getting softer. I know what she's telling me. I had used my power before, not knowing what I was doing, not knowing what could happen, but not caring at all about me but just about Lily and only to find her, not to fix what happened or make it better. Just to find her and I didn't go all the way. I just made it easier for her to find me. That was the right thing to do and this was the right thing to do, too, saving Missy but nothing more, not taking away her hurt and not trying to fix anything else.

"I won't forget, I promise," I tell Crocodile.

"That's good because I like this Alligator, not the other bonehead you are sometimes," she smiles.

"I don't like that bonehead, either." I answer.

"One more thing," she's rooting around in a pocket of her dress, her eyes far away and her tongue half out in concentration. "I've got something for you... right... right... no...wait... right here!"

She holds out a small, shiny crystal in her hand, a crystal I got to hold three times before—once when I was in love with Lily and wanted to be with her forever and once when I wanted to use my power just like Amara showed me, so I was breaking the crystal in chunks and throwing them away because it felt amazing to have that kind of power and use it. And the last time was when I helped Devi make Lily human. I had crushed the crystal in my hands and spread the little crystal dust into Shane Lake. Wiped it all off my hands.

"Well, come on," she scolds me. "Take it."

I take it carefully, wondering if Lily is somehow going to appear or the crystal will light up or something goofy like that when I touch it. Of course, it doesn't. It just sits there in my hand, cool and quiet, and I just sit here on the bench, Missy slumped against me, staring at this crystal dumbly.

"You could say thank you, you know," Crocodile says, shaking her head and rolling her eyes at me.

"Yeah...yeah, sure. Thanks, Crocodile," I say, looking quickly back at the crystal, my mouth still full of confusion.

"Oh, that didn't sound like you mean it," she scolds, putting her hands on her hips. "Your mom and dad taught you better manners than that."

I close my hand around the crystal and pull it to my chest. I look at Crocodile, who is watching me closely, waiting for my proper appreciation.

"I know you don't give presents that often or to many people—" I start.

"Just you," she cuts in, impatiently.

I ignore her and keep going.

"—and I really like being one of your friends—"

"Just you," she jumps in again.

"—so thank you for this really nice gift. It means a lot to me, coming from you."

Her eyes and face light up to go with her huge smile.

"Can I put it on you? Please? Please?" She's so excited she can't stand still.

"What—what do you mean?" I'm all confused again. This can't be Lily's essence because I destroyed that so what is this thing I'm holding?

Crocodile comes up to me and points at my closed hand.

"Look closely at it, silly," she says. "It's got a chain around it, so you can wear it around your neck."

I put my hand down from my chest and uncurl my fingers. Sure enough, there's a thin, delicate silver chain running through a little loop in one corner of the crystal. Before I can think about it too much, Crocodile reaches forward and plucks the crystal out of my hand.

"You're so slow, like we've got all day. Some of us are busy, you know," she says, unclasping the chain so she's holding the two ends in either hand, with the crystal dangling in between, catching the light from the sun in colourful bursts inside.

She steps up to me and I lean forward, putting my head down so she can reach around and attach the two ends together, which she does quickly.

"Sit up now, let's see how it looks," she orders.

I sit back and feel the weight of it of the chain on my

neck. With my free hand, I feel the crystal resting against my chest. There's no energy or anything coming from it. It just feels like a crystal. I'll have time to figure this out later. Crocodile is talking so I look up at her.

"Oh, yeah, that looks great," she says, nodding. "And don't you worry about that chain—it's just like me, little and super strong, it'll never come off."

The sound of that scares me but I just give a short laugh and a nervous smile.

"This is really nice," I somehow say and sound okay. "Thanks a lot."

She stands there looking at me and the smile is slowly sliding off her face. She's waiting for something. I'm supposed to offer her something more but I can't think what. She's looking down now and I can tell she's quite sad all of a sudden. I'm not sure how I can figure it out. Maybe it's Missy slumped against me, my other arm around her shoulders, that reminds me what I should do. This is just a little girl and she needs more than a thanks.

"Hey, Crocodile," I say, holding my other arm out. She looks up, her lip quivering. She'll be crying soon. "Come over here. Let me give you a hug."

Her sad and unhappy face is gone in a flash, replaced by her smile again. She steps forward slow and shy, glancing at the ground. I put my free arm around her and pull her in, squeezing her. She's tense at first and then relaxes but she keeps her arms at her side.

"I guess you don't get a lot of hugs," I say, patting her back.

"Just you," she answers softly.

"You can have a hug from me anytime you want, not just when you bring me stuff," I say, giving her an extra squeeze to show I mean it.

"Really?" she says, turning her face to look at me. Because she's standing, we're at the same height.

"Really really," I smile back.

She throws her arms around my neck and squeezes me so tight that it feels like I can't breathe for a second.

"I love you," she says into my ear, her voice loud and excited. "You're the best."

Before I can react, she lets go.

"Well, I gotta run but don't be a stranger, okay?"

I still can't say anything and she's already strolling away down the path.

"See you later, Alligator," she calls out, not looking back.

"In a while, Crocodile," I finally manage to say, before she disappears.

Missy sits up, startled.

She looks at me, confused, and then she smiles.

"Nice, real nice," she says, looking at me and then at the crystal on my chest.

Blood on the floor (Kathy)

I've always had this ability to make small talk and I seem to be able to turn it on when I need it the most. When I'm ready to blow up inside with what I really want to say, my mouth goes on automatic but in a good way. There I am, asking about the weather, the job, the clothes, the music, the latest online sensation or the price of food in the Middle East and how it is leading to social unrest. I can do it for the most serious or the most silly of topics.

It's a gift I inherited from mom, who mastered it at work, I guess, although when I asked her about it once, not that long ago, she just laughed and said she got used to doing it with "your father."

Then she looked at me more seriously and said: "I shouldn't talk about your dad that way, Kathryn, but here's some woman-to-woman advice. There are some men that are hard to reach but once you get passed the bullshit, they're wonderful, and there are some men who are nothing more than bullshit."

"I take it Dad's the bullshit?" I asked.

She looked at me like that was a stupid question and we moved on to whatever else we were doing at the time. Dad is a corporate executive in the energy sector in Calgary and makes more in a month than Mom does in a year, even at what she makes. He sends money to Mom to satisfy their divorce but Mom has had full custody of us since I was 10 and Jill was 5. He would come visit and then that became just phone calls and then nothing at all. I haven't talked to him in five years and seen him in nearly seven.

And then there's Alex, just getting up to clear the table. There's a guy who can turn on the bullshit even better than Mom (he is a lawyer so I guess that's what lawyers do—argue points they don't agree with but act like they do, like in debate club) but you can tell he really cares about things and people. I start to get up to help him.

"Kathy, you wounded yourself making my dinner. How about you sit there and I'll clean up, okay?"

Jill is asking mom if she can go over to a friend's down the road to work on a project for school so Mom is already up and encouraging her out the door. So while Alex is clearing the dishes and Mom is pushing Jill out the door, I get up and slip into the living room. The box with the gold bars and papers is under an end table by the window and the paintings are upside down on the coffee table. The only time Jill and I are ever in this room is when Mom has visitors or when she needs to talk to one or both of us about something serious, which isn't too often.

I can already see Jill walking down the street with her backpack and I can hear Mom with Alex in the kitchen but I can't hear what they're saying as they scrape out food from pans into plastic containers while plates and cutlery get placed in the dishwasher.

I pull the box out and tug it across the floor to the loveseat so I only have to lift it up once, since it's so heavy. I move the paintings so they're beside me on the end table and I put the laptop on the coffee table. Just as I sit down, Mom and Alex come into the living room. Mom quickly reads where she and Alex are supposed to sit, so she guides him to the couch directly across from me, with the coffee table between us.

Alex takes a sip from his scotch then puts the glass down on the end table beside him, making sure to lay down a coaster first.

"So you're going to tell me what's going on, Kathy, right? Because your mom won't give me any hints," he says, smirking at her to make sure she understands he's only teasing.

When he looks at me and I don't answer right away, his smile slips away. He looks at both of us and quickly sees how serious we both are. He's about to open his mouth to say something so I get started.

"Alex, Mom and I need some advice and it's not just advice from a friend but legal advice, too."

Mom sits back calmly in the sofa and rests her hand on Alex's shoulder. She's watching me closely to see if she needs to help out, in case I can't hold it together. She's watching his reactions, too.

"Okay," Alex says, glancing over to Mom before looking back at me. "Normally, I would make a joke here about an after-hours consultation and I bill $500 an hour, minimum four hours, but this seems more serious."

"Mom," I say, looking at her. "Could you show Alex the letter from Lily to me on the laptop?"

Mom grabs the laptop, opens it and makes a few clicks. Alex wants to watch her but he focuses on me as I talk.

"You know about the cops looking at Lily, about those letters she sent to those people about the murders. After she died but before they got here, I hid some of Lily's things, including this laptop. I know I could get into trouble for doing that but just read the letter, and then Mom will show you the actual letters Lily sent and some other things on the laptop."

Mom holds out the laptop to him but he doesn't take it. Instead, he takes his scotch and stands up. He steps a few feet away from her, takes a much bigger sip of his scotch, swallows carefully and then turns to face both of us. I don't need to be his boyfriend to know he's trying to hold in how mad he is.

"Tonya, close that laptop and get it out of my sight right now," he says, firmly to Mom but he's not even looking at her. He's glaring at me. "Congratulations, Kathy, you've made your mother an accessory to your crime of impeding a police investigation and obstructing justice. And if you've benefited in any financial way from anything in that box or those pictures, you may also be guilty of profiting from the proceeds of crime. Depending on the seriousness of the crimes, and from what you and your mom have told me, Lily linked herself to four murders, so you're looking at years, not months, in jail if a court found you guilty."

Mom had set the laptop in her lap and listened politely but now she cuts in. I'm too much in shock to think or feel anything.

"So you can't even look at this with us and help us understand it?" she asks, a frustrated edge to her voice.

Alex takes another step backwards. He's not so mad now but he's firm and direct.

"If I did and then didn't turn it over to the police, knowing that it is an item sought in a police investigation, I would be disbarred and then I'd be an accessory, just like you, Tonya. So here's what's going to happen—I'm going to my car to get my briefcase since this is a professional call. While I'm gone, you two will put away all of that well out of my sight. When I get back, you'll *TELL* me, not show me, what you have. And the last 90 seconds never happened."

He doesn't wait for either of us to answer. He's already out of the room and down the hall. Mom's on her feet, not trying anymore to hide how upset she is.

"For Christ's sake, we're asking for help, not a goddamn law class," she mutters, but she's already bending down and pushing the laptop under the couch. From her knees, she looks back up at me.

"C'mon, Kathy," she says, more gently. "Pass me the paintings. Let's get through this."

I snap out of it because it's easier to listen and obey and do something then to try and process everything. After I hand her the paintings, she carefully places them one by one under the couch with the laptop.

"Could you move the box into the hall closet? Just slide it in beside the winter boots and close the door," she tells me.

I hurry with the box, even though it's so heavy. As I'm closing the door, I can hear Alex coming back up the steps. For some reason, I run back into the living room and sit beside Mom. She smiles and puts her arm around my shoulder, pulling me close.

"It's going to be okay. I won't let anything bad happen to you," she reassures me.

"But, Mom—" I'm trying not to cry and Alex is coming back in and sitting down on the couch opposite from us, where I had been sitting before. "I'm scared."

Mom chews her lip for a second and then moves in for a hug.

"Me, too, Pumpkin. Me, too."

She lets go of me but takes my hand when we turn to face Alex. Both of us are sitting on the edge of the cushion, tense. Alex has a small notepad in his lap and a pen in his hand.

"Okay," he says, friendly but professional, looking at me. "Tell me about the letter on the laptop from Lily that was addressed to you specifically and then tell me everything that's happened since."

So I talk and Mom steers me, helping me keep things in the right order. She disappears a couple of times, once to bring me a Coke and tea for her and Alex, although his goes cold and he doesn't touch it. He barely lifts his head, writing the whole time. When Jill comes home, Mom urges us to go downstairs to keep talking where we won't be heard while she spends some time with Jill, leading her upstairs. I put the TV on, in case Jill did wander downstairs and ask why I was just sitting here talking with Alex by myself, which is something I would normally never do but I might watch TV with him if I liked the show.

I'm getting paranoid, making sure there's an excuse or a reason for everything.

There's not much left to tell anyway except for today and Mom comes down and sits cross-legged on the floor just as I'm finishing. Jill must have gone to bed. Oh, wow, it's already past 10, I notice on the clock on the PVR. I've been talking for more than two hours.

Nobody says anything while he makes more notes and begins flipping back and forth in his notepad. Finally, he looks up.

"Okay, this isn't as bad as I thought," he says. "I'm going to ask a few questions and then I'd like to see everything you have but we can deal with that tomorrow since it's getting late. For starters, don't worry about the letters since there's no way Lily could have been at three of those murders and the fourth one, she would have been so young as to not be legally responsible. I'm presuming at this point that both of you have been the victims of an elaborate hoax, in terms of the gold bars and everything else, which is why I'll want to see that and then that locker."

"But it's true!" I shout, jumping to my feet. "I'll go get it and show you."

Alex has his hand up and Mom is shushing me to be quiet.

"Kathy, we'll consider both the possible and the impossible but first, let's start with a hoax as being the most reasonable explanation," he says, soft but firm. "Please sit."

I sit down with my arms crossed, glaring at him. Like mom, he'll need to see for himself before he believes it, believes Lily has been living all this time and has all this stuff and was running from other people like her.

"We're wasting time here when we could be trying to use this stuff to maybe find Sam," I grumble.

Alex starts nodding.

"Sam is the missing piece, I agree, but I see it a little differently than you," he says, leaning forward and staring at me. "Sam has managed to disappear with nothing but the clothes on his back, as far as the police and his parents are concerned. That's impossible without a lot of resources that no one knew about. How do you know Sam didn't take his money from that account at the credit union and run when he found out Lily died?"

I look away, shaking my head.

"Why would Sam do that and put his parents, put me, through all of this?" I manage to get out before I can feel the tears coming. I don't move except to keep my face turned from Alex and Mom. I swallow hard a few times and blink to keep it down.

"Only Sam can answer that and he's not here so let's move on," Alex states calmly. "It's not just Sam who has disappeared but Lily's dad Bodie is gone, too. And there are no formal records for her mom under the name she gave everyone here. Same for Lily, even here at KLO high school, even at the high school in Ottawa where she says she went and met that teacher who was killed."

"That's why we have to go to Paris, to meet that lawyer and find out," I said, a desperate whine in my voice. "That's the only thing we've got."

Alex glances over at Mom and they exchange a look for a quick second and then Alex gets up and comes to sit beside me. I recognize that look because I've seen it before, but when Jill is doing or saying something and Alex wants to intervene but doesn't want to step on Mom's toes as the parent. Mom not saying anything is her way of giving Alex permission to talk to me as if he was my Dad for a minute.

He gives me lots of space and he doesn't try to touch me with some reassuring pat on the shoulder or arm or leg or anything like that. He lets his voice, gentle but firm, try to reach me. I won't look at him. I'm staring at the back wall above where he was sitting a minute ago.

"Kathy, I have three kinds of advice I want to give you and then I'm going to go home and you can talk to your Mom and decide what you're going to do. I'm flattered you shared this problem with me but I also know you told me more because of my job than because I'm me and I'm good with that. So here's my first piece of advice and that comes from my job."

He looks over to include mom and alternates back and forth between talking to me and talking to her.

"Legally, you should bring everything you have from Lily to the Kelowna police right now, including the keys to the storage locker. Tonight. Tell them everything. You both may later face criminal charges for what you've done and you might face more charges if they think that you're still holding back. I don't believe you would go to jail for those charges but the police and the court could make your lives pretty uncomfortable and house arrest isn't as wonderful as it sounds in the media."

"I thought you'd say that," Mom says, looking at me. "What else?"

"Personally, I don't like Lily and I've never met her. She's asked you to do things, some of them explicitly, like going to see this lawyer, and some unintentionally perhaps, like lie to the police, that are unreasonable requests as far as I'm concerned but that's your decision to make, not mine. I believe in standing by my friends, too, but this is too much."

I'm still not looking at him and now I'm biting my lip and shaking my head slowly. I'm already planning how I'm going to convince Mom to let me go on my own to Paris. Alex is a nice guy and I'll thank him when all of this is over but he doesn't get it.

"I find your story hard to believe and I think the two of you have been tricked but the fact that what the two of you have seen has convinced you both, I'm willing to put my disbelief aside as much as I can. So here's what I think you should do, Kathy."

He pauses. He's cut Mom out of the conversation and he's focusing just on me. I take a quick glance at him sideways and then I stare at the floor. Mom comes over and sits with me, her hand on my arm, but I don't look at her either.

"I think you should get up early tomorrow, call the lawyer in Paris and invite him to come to Kelowna. Send him scanned copies of the letters. Tell him you cannot to travel to Paris because it would look suspicious to the police and because you're needed here in case Sam is… found," he lingers on that word long enough to make sure I get the "dead or alive" part that he's not saying after.

"What if he can't come?" I ask, finally looking at him. I've ditched the whine and I sound like a grownup again. "What if he won't come?"

Alex smiles and finally reaches forward to pat me on the knee.

"Kathy, if he knows half as much about Lily as what you've told me, he'll be on the next plane to Canada. If he doesn't come, I'll buy you that plane ticket to Paris. How's that sound?"

I'm trying to hold in my smile but I can't. I just nod

and keep staring at the floor. I feel so tired but I know I won't be able to sleep until I talk to that lawyer.

"How many hours are they ahead of us?" I ask, not caring if either of them answer me. "I'm calling tonight."

Making it all better (Missy)

Well, look who's here and saved the day.

I give Sam a real big hug to show my appreciation and everything and then jump to my feet. He feels different. He looks different. That's sure a nice little crystal hanging around his neck. Very pretty. I wonder who gave it to him or when he got it. He didn't have it the last time I saw him or anytime before that.

And now I'm not so sure I'm all that happy with him.

"You sure took your time stopping her, you know. What's the deal with that?"

I don't want to be ungrateful or anything because I know that Sara girl, his little sister, was ready to kill me for good, but Sam seemed to take his sweet old time helping me out. Like he wasn't sure that saving me from her was the right thing to do, when it's so obvious it was.

He's on his feet now, too, and his arms are open and he's stepping forward to give me a big hug. His face is sad and apologetic. I get up from the bench and I let him do it because that's the last thing for him to do, to hug me, to bring me close to him without being scared or mad or anything else. He holds me close and doesn't let go and I feel really safe. I squeeze him back tight and he doesn't try to stop me or step away.

"I'm sorry, I'm really sorry," he says.

This is why he's different.

Right up until he stopped his sister from killing me, he

couldn't have done this. But he stopped his sister without hurting her. He even let her have the satisfaction first of feeling like she had killed him. Then he put her back in the time where she belongs. I don't know how he's doing all that—letting himself die and moving through time—but I'm going to ask Cam, for sure.

Here he comes up the path now and he's looking at me and I can tell how proud he is of me.

"Oh, Cam," I breathe. "Everything gonna be okay."

To know I did the right thing and I got through it all and to have him let me know I did what I was supposed to and stayed strong, that's what makes it all worthwhile.

I give Sam one more hard squeeze because it's time for me to go.

"Hey, I'm Sam, not Cam," he says, squeezing back and then letting go when I do.

"I know that now," I say, standing back so I can see him. He really does look a lot better now. "But right after you saved me, you really felt like him for a second, the way you hugged me and made me feel safe."

"Oh," he says, a little confused. "Well then, who's Cam?"

"He's Cam to me but everyone else calls him Cameron and he's right behind you," I answer.

Sam turns but not fast and tense. I walk up to stand beside Sam as my old buddy comes up to us and stops.

"Hello, Missy, I'm glad to see you are well," Cam says, smiling at me.

"I take a licking and keep on ticking," I smile back. "And it's nice to see you, too. I thought for a few seconds there that I'd never see you again." I put my hand on Sam's shoulder. "But Sam here saved the day and I can't thank him enough for that. I was lucky again," I say.

Cam looks at Sam and I can tell Sam is seeing him for the first time but he's not trying to figure out what he is or anything. He seems really calm and relaxed. He's here and nowhere else.

"Thank you for saving my friend," Cam says. "I know that must have been difficult for you."

"It—I—Ummm…" He's tripping over his words like a kid so he looks over at me instead. "It was the right thing to do," he finally says, more to me than to Cam.

I smile back.

"I have to go now, Sam, because I'm done here and everything and I think you and Cam are going to have a little visit for a bit," I say, letting go of his shoulder and sliding over towards Cam.

I'm still a little nervous to tell him this so I'm hoping being beside Cam will help in case there's any trouble. I take a deep breath and just say it.

"One of the places I have to go, Sam, is with your mom and dad. They're really hurting again since Lily died and you went away and I should be with them, you know," I say, standing straight and staring at him right in the face.

He just looks at me and doesn't say anything but I can tell he's not mad. He's just remembering that he promised to kill me if I ever went near them again. I managed to stay away this long because I had to be with Sam and I wanted to help him out best I could but I really have to go to them now.

"Could I take you there? I'd like to go with you, if that's alright with you," he says, all humble and quiet. "I'd understand if you said no."

Wow, I wasn't expecting that.

"Yeah, but I'm going right now and I know you want

to talk to Cam and everything," I tell him back. "I know how to get there, you know."

He smiles softly, just with his lips, still quiet and nice. Boy, if he would have talked to me like this not long ago, I would have wondered what he was up to or if he was gonna try to kill me or something after we leave Cam here but before we got to his mom and dad.

Cam says nothing beside me, waiting for Sam's answer.

"I can talk to Cameron later, in a little while," Sam says.

"You'll still be here, right?" he adds, looking away from me and over at Cameron.

"Yes, of course," Cameron says back, making his way over to the bench and sitting down. "This is where Missy comes to find me and you can find me here, too."

I run over and bend down to give Cam a big hug.

"Okay, I'll see you later," I squeeze him. "Sorry for the hi and goodbye but I've got stuff to do."

"That's fine, my dear," he pats me with one hand on the back of my shoulder. "I'll be with you again soon."

"Awesome," I stand up and turn back to Sam. "You ready?"

"Yeah, sure," he answers back.

And we're gone.

The fourth reply

Victim Impact Statement From Lynette Jamieson
From the records of the Ottawa Police Service, Service De Police D'Ottawa
Gary's disappearance in 1999—AND NOW I'M TOLD MURDER—left me with three kids under 10, no

life insurance except for his pension plan, that would have only been enough to bury him, except THERE WAS NO BODY TO BURY and the Ontario Teachers Pension Nazis wouldn't pay the life insurance because THERE WAS NO BODY TO BURY!!!!!!!! Even after seven years, they said they would take it to court because there was no proof that he hadn't run off with some other woman.

I had to sell the house Gary and his dad built after we got married because I couldn't keep the mortgage, pay all the bills, on just my hairdresser pay. Me and the three kids ended up in a tiny 3-bedroom apartment and I had to take a second job on weekends, just to put food on the table. Gary's mom looked after the kids as much as she could and always brought over casseroles and food—made me feel like a charity even though she was so nice and Gary's dad came over and always did little repair things, like screwing the boy's bunk beds together better so they would stop squeaking. My family was USELESS, of course!—but I expected that. My loser older sister Linda even had the unbelievable nerve to call me a few months after Gary disappeared and I was packing to move out and not offer to help but to ASK FOR MONEY! On top of the $2,000 she already owed me from the two times me and Gary lent her money before!!!!!!

I put my whole life on hold to raise my kids—there was no boyfriend, a few nights out with some girlfriends here and there when Gary's mom and dad took the kids out to the farm during the weekend in the summer but I had to get my friends to pay for my drinks or I couldn't go—SO HUMILIATING!!!! But I did it and now my kids are in school and working and doing well but they cried their eyes out with me when we first lost Gary but I never wondered if Gary just ran off with someone—I knew something happened to him because he loved me and loved his family and we loved him.

The Ontario Teachers Pension Assholes only recently sent me a cheque for Gary's life insurance, except at the rate for 1999, not the rate for today WHICH IS $15,000 MORE, because they said since Gary died in 1999, that's what they have to pay to be fair to the other teachers, and not pay today's rate, even though they didn't pay in 1999, they're paying today! I want to sue them but I'd have to use Gary's life insurance to hire a lawyer and for what? But I could sure use that money to help my kids through school and I have no pension and just Gary's pension from the stupid teachers and a little bit in RSPs that we put in before I lost Gary.

I've got arthritis in my hands from 25 years of cutting hair 40-50 hours a week and my knees, my hips and my feet are always sore. I've been out on some dates my friends have set up but I can't believe some of the losers they've introduced to me, especially the ones that knew Gary. Gary was the best thing that ever happened to me so why would I settle for some uneducated guy with a rusty car, bad breath and barely a pot to piss in? I'm so LONELY but there's no way EVER that I'll be with a man who wouldn't have been good enough to shine Gary's shoes.

I have a little more money now because I don't have 3 mouths at home to feed and now I have this life insurance money but I'm going to pay some bills with that and help my kids. It's already spent. I still rent a place—it's not the best but it's comfortable. Some days I'm even happy.

And then the letter came and I couldn't believe it so I took the bus down to Elgin Street, feeling sick because I used to go down to see the police every month, then every

3 months, then once a year to ask about Gary and I realized I hadn't asked about him in FOUR YEARS!!!!!!! And they took the letter and said they'd get back to me. And then they called that night and they had the bones that had been CHEWED UP BY ANIMALS!!!!!!!!! When his body was just dumped there, in the middle of the bush, like GARBAGE!!!!!!

They're still waiting for the DNA tests to make sure it's him but I know it I KNOW IT'S HIM. I read that letter and it sounded like so many of the letters I got when Gary disappeared from his students and even old students he first taught 10 years before. I felt a little sorry for this girl Lily for having a mom like that and I can't imagine what kind of mess she's in but now I just don't care. I want to hold my kids and I want to bury my husband.

A detour with Missy (Sam)

I think about changes over time as I walk with Missy along Abbott Street, across Harvey Avenue and into that scenic part of historic Kelowna, where Kelowna's old money and new money meet, where the longtime rich and well-known Kelowna families live in their well-kept heritage houses next to the new rich who came from Vancouver or Calgary and knew enough about Kelowna that the rich belong here, not in the Mission or along the side of a golf course, but right here, not far from downtown and the highway, tucked along the lake, not far from the hospital. It's so easy to see the contrast between the houses that have been here since before the Second World War and the newer, gaudier mansions crammed onto the tiny lots.

We're walking here and now but no one can see us.

Missy does have physical form with me but I don't think she or Cameron could actually be seen by anyone so I imitate them. I'm right here and completely out of sight, just like Bodie asked, but I'm not completely out of sight, am I? I can still be seen by guardians and that makes me wonder. Bodie stressed the word—completely—because maybe it's important to be completely out of sight, not just from humans but from guardians, too. But where could I go where I could do that? I don't know about a place where even guardians don't know about or can't go.

For any guardians, in the past or present, I can maybe be invisible from them but I think they'd still be able to sense me, they'd still know someone was around and just by how it felt, they'd know it was me. I went through the past and watched Lily kill people and protect Cindy but she didn't know I was there because I didn't stay long. I was casually flipping pages, stopping at the interesting points in a long, thick book. The one time I really stopped and looked at her, back at the very beginning, she could feel me there, I could tell, so I stepped back.

Missy hasn't said a word but now I notice she's taking these quick glances over at me from time to time but at my chest, at the crystal hanging there. I've been trying to ignore it, letting the idea of it hanging around my neck hopefully just sink in. I can feel the weight of it on me, which doesn't match the size of it. It's heavier than it should be but it's still comfortable. She's noticed that I've caught her looking at it, so I start talking, which isn't a bad thing. Maybe talking about it will help me figure it out.

"It represents Lily, you know, but that's all. It's not really her. It's just there to remind me of her, as if I'd every forget," I say.

"That's pretty nice," she says, smiling. "But who gave it to you? You didn't have it before."

"Do you know...um...well, her nickname is Crocodile to me and she doesn't want me to call her anything else but I know Bodie called her Camille. Do you know her? She's a—"

I glance over and Missy is still smiling but this is one of those "knowing smiles" that the guy in that writing seminar I took in Spokane told me I shouldn't ever use because "knowing smile" is a cliché. I've got a better phrase to describe it now. It's a Bodie smile but in Missy's style. Bodie used to smile like that a lot at me when I started to describe something or someone to him, forgetting he already knew pretty much everything and everyone.

"What?" I ask Missy. "Do you know her?"

Her smile doesn't drop.

"If there's a guardian who knows sweet little Camille, that would be me," she says. "I like to think of myself as her big sister, you know, sorta like Cindy was for Lily. So, I have two Cams—Cameron and Camille—and they are really special to me."

She pauses for a second and then her voice drops.

"Although I am kinda scared of Camille, sometimes, because of what she does, you know. I don't really see the others much, well, I saw Lily and Cindy sometimes, when they were with us," she looks at me carefully, hoping she's not hurting my feelings.

I ignore the reference to Lily and ask another question, to get Missy to talk more about Crocodile.

"How do you know Croco...sorry, Camille...so well?" I ask.

"Well, when living things are really hurting, that's where I come in, you know," she says, waving her arms around in explanation. "So, either I'm with that thing for the rest of its life, or they find a way past me, like you did, and then Cameron comes into their life and they forgive themselves, maybe not totally but enough that they can keep going, or they decide they can't take me anymore and then I take them to Camille. Well, I do that for the first thing, too, I guess, but it takes longer."

"I bet they're happy to see her, too, after spending time with you." I should have stopped at just the first part but the second part comes flying out of my mouth before I can stop it and I realize right away how mean it sounds. I turn to apologize but she waves me off.

"Oh, you don't have to be that way," she says and I can tell she's not upset. "Of course they're happy to see her. She's so cute and I'm…well, it's not that I'm not cute but people feel bad when I'm around. That's what I do, you know."

We turn left off Abbott onto Cadder Avenue and I get an idea as I look up the street and see the traffic from Pandosy Street.

"That corner up there, Missy, have you been there before?" I ask.

She looks ahead and shrugs her shoulders.

"I dunno, I've been everywhere before," she answers. "Well, everywhere there are living things that hurt. And don't get me off topic—I hate it when Cameron does that to me—are you saying Camille gave you that nice crystal thing around your neck?"

I feel its weight pulling on the chain around my neck and how it sits heavy against my chest, even though I'm standing. I have this huge temptation to touch it but I stop my hand before it gets there, concentrating on answering Missy instead.

"She did give it to me and I do want to talk about it and I want to go see my parents with you but are you okay with us taking a little side trip?" I ask, raising my voice as an older truck in need of a tuneup goes along Pandosy. We're getting near the corner and the traffic light.

"It won't take long, I promise," I add. "Then we'll talk about the crystal Camille gave me and we'll go see my parents."

She notices the street corner and now she's looking at me, her eyes wide and nervous.

"I remember now," she says, stopping at the corner. She's looking down at her feet. "I remember the last time I stood here. Well, it was over there," she adds, pointing to the opposite corner, "but I was here."

"Show me, Missy," I say, holding out my hand to her, hoping she'll take it. "Please."

She looks at my hand and then my face.

"You don't need me for this," she says, shaking her head.

"I know, but I'd like it if you came along," I answer, keeping my hand out to her. "It would mean a lot to me. I need to see it. I need to know."

She looks away from my face and back to my hand.

She reaches for it, then stops.

"This doesn't hurt or anything, right? Going back like this?" she asks, looking at me concerned.

"I promise it won't," I smile.

She takes my hand and I keep smiling at her.

She smiles back but I can tell how scared she is as the time falls away from us.

She closes her eyes so I squeeze her hand harder and pull her closer, hoping that makes her feel a little better.

Back where Sam began (Missy)

We go back further than the street corner but it doesn't really matter, anyway, since even then I was already with Albert, Sam's grandfather, but everyone called him Al because he was a nice man, so maybe I should call him Al, too.

I joined Al after his wife Beatrice (everybody called her Betty, even though she wasn't an Elizabeth) died in the hospital just down the street from here. I was there with him at her death bed. Before that, he honestly thought she'd beat the cancer but on her last day, it finally came to him and he was really hurting. He cried hard for a long time. He was so hurt I thought he wouldn't last the night before killing himself.

Art and Anna, Sam's mom and dad, were there at the hospital, too, and they kept poor Al alive, although they didn't know it. What a sweet young couple, so in love. They had been married for three years but they acted like it was three minutes. Art loved Al even more than he loved his own father and Anna worshipped her dad so it was pretty easy for them to really focus on Al and take care of him. They took him to their home and he stayed there, in a bedroom they made up in the basement next to the laundry room.

This was 10 months before Sam was born.

When Art and Anna found out about the pregnancy, they were so happy. They had been trying for a long time and they were starting to wonder if something was wrong.

Sam is not spying on his parents conceiving him or anything gross like that but he slows this moment down and is waiting for Amara.

"Where's Amara? Shouldn't she be here?" he asks me, a little frustrated.

"She is here, Sam," I say, motioning downstairs with my head. We're still holding hands.

We don't walk down the stairs. Sam just takes us there, like pressing down on the handle of one of those old Viewmaster toys, to advance the wheel of pictures to the next picture. Now we're in the room with Al and it's bright and Amara was here. And I was here, too, so I'm here twice—me here with Sam, holding hands, and me over there with Amara, too, with Al, back then.

Al couldn't see us yet but he knew we were there, me and Amara. He was doing and saying all the right things during the day when Art and Anna were around but at night he would come down here and he was starting to go crazy.

"He is the one for this mission," Amara told me. I didn't say anything because I had no idea what she was talking about or what she was doing there. Now I get it, of course. Would have got into a fight with her right there if I had known then what I know now.

"I did not find him. I felt him reaching out to me. He was looking for me," she said.

I look over at Sam and he's nodding but I don't ask him what he's thinking. He's figuring it all out and that's good.

When Art and Anna told Al that they were expecting a little baby, Al was happy but they thought he was happy for them. He was happy because Amara was with him when he was alone at night, shining her light on him, making him feel better. He was tearing himself apart because he was hurting more than ever at the same time, because he really missed Betty and felt his life was for nothing.

So he started painting in the basement and Art and

Anna and her brother would sometimes go down there and see what he was up to and praise Al and encourage him to do more. He started losing weight but he was pretty chubby to begin with so everyone thought that was a good thing, at least at first. But then the paintings got different and, even back then, I could see what me and Amara were doing to his brain. I didn't ask Amara what she was hanging around for because I didn't know anything and I was polite but I was curious so I just waited and watched.

Just like I'm watching now, again, here with Sam.

"How could I have been so foolish?" Amara was raving while Al was painting away. He was freaking Art and Anna out at the end when he would paint in the dark but because he could see Amara's light, he wasn't in the dark, but he was as far as any human person could see.

"Just because this human male could sense me does not mean he was the one for my plan."

"Umm…I'm just here to check in on Al and he does seem happier, although he's now pretty scared," I answered her back but Amara is already turning away from me so I left, thinking I didn't like her much. I saw Al only one more time after that. I hope Sam doesn't go there, too, but I think he might.

But this time, I'm staying here watching with Sam. Now Bodie came in. I didn't know until now he came after I left.

"Have you come here to tell me more riddles?" she shouted at him. "I require answers, not mysterious lectures."

"Amara," he said. "Look at the paintings. He is telling you what to do."

Sam takes in a sharp breath beside me because now

he's properly looking at the paintings, too. All Al was painting, over and over, were portraits of pregnant Anna and inside her belly there is always a black circle. With each painting, the focus is more on the belly and the black circle. This last painting is just a black circle with the red of the womb in the corners.

"The baby is dark, the baby is dark," Al muttered, standing back.

"He said it best," Bodie added, turning to Amara.

Al turned around.

"I said what best?" he said, staring straight at Bodie.

Sam squeezes my hand and I squeeze back so he doesn't do anything stupid. He wants to make it stop and he knows he could but it's not the right thing. He has to watch and just watch.

"The baby is dark," Bodie replies. "You are correct."

Al nodded and then looked at Amara.

"You look even lovelier than I imagined," he said, lowering his eyes. "But I can't look at you for more than a second because you're too bright."

Amara looks at Al, then looks at Bodie. She has a black marble in her hand but she hesitates. She still doesn't know what to do with it.

Al looked up and saw the marble in Amara's hand. His faces twisted, his eyes went wide. He spun around, grabbing a couple of small knives stained with paint that I remember seeing him use to cut open little paint tins. He turned back to Bodie and Amara, his eyes burning and his face all in pain.

"I WON'T DO IT! I WON'T DO IT!" he shouted at them. "I WON'T!"

He ran past them, charging up the stairs. Amara moved to follow but Bodie caught her arm.

"Wait," he commanded.

She looked at him, confused.

They listened.

And we're listening too, as Al started to attack Anna upstairs.

Sam starts for the stairs but I pull him back.

"Wait," I tell him, knowing I don't sound as impressive and smart as Bodie.

But he stops.

And we listen.

Anna screamed and screamed and Al was shouting at her.

"Don't you understand? There's a monster inside of you!"

"What—" Art came in from outside.

"I won't let you stop me!" Al yelled, and we could hear his stomping feet, charging across the floor at Art.

They grunted and fought while Anna just kept screaming.

"Stop it, Al! Stop!" Art begged, all breathless and grunting.

A door opened hard upstairs, slamming into the wall, shaking the glass in it.

"Get out! Get out!" Art shouted.

The sound of the fighting ended. Anna was still screaming but it turned all ragged.

"Honey, honey! He's gone! It's okay!" he said to her. "Oh, God!"

Anna stopped screaming suddenly.

"Stay with me, honey! STAY WITH ME!" Art cried.

He ran into the next room.

"Now?" Amara said, looking at Bodie.

"Yes," Bodie answered.

Me and Sam follow them up the stairs. I let go of his hand and put my arms around his shoulders, pulling him close to me so we can both fit in the doorway.

There was blood everywhere but it was all centred on his mom, who was slumped on the floor against a cupboard door, her legs spread out in front of her. Her eyes were closed but she was moaning as she pulled in shallow little breaths through her mouth. Her arms and hands were cut and there was one long cut on her belly, through her summer dress, but it wasn't deep.

Bodie was standing off to the side but his eyes were wide and he was staring, like he was seeing something for the first time and wanted to make sure he remembered every little bit of it. Amara crouched down beside Anna, staring at her belly and then at her face.

She looked back up at Bodie but he didn't say anything. Her face looked like she didn't know what to do next and wanted him to tell her.

"You cannot force this on her, Amara, and you only have a few more seconds. Her husband will be back shortly," he said.

Art was in the hallway, shouting into the phone.

"TWENTY-TWO FIFTY-FIVE WOODLAWN STRE—… NO, NO, NO, TWO, TWO, FIVE, FIVE WOODLAWN…THAT'S RIGHT…FIVE-FIVE, WOODLAWN STREET…GOOD LORD, I COULD CARRY HER MYSELF TO THE HOSPITAL FROM HERE, I'M TWO BLOCKS AWAY…OKAY, OKAY, I'M SORRY BUT HE ATTACKED HER AND SHE'S BLEEDING AND SHE'S EIGHT MONTHS PREGNANT!"

Amara turned back to Anna, holding out the black marble to her in her open hand.

"Anna Gardner," Amara said, softly and with respect. It looked like she was trying not to cry. "Please take this from me and give it to your unborn son. Please bring my Samael back to me. Please."

Anna opened her eyes slowly, until they were halfway open. She was groggy and she didn't look at Amara but she saw the hand and the marble in front of her. She took it and pressed Amara's closed hand against her chest. She sighed.

"My Sam…my Sam…my Sam…my Sam…," she said, but then it changed.

Something happened.

"My…oh…Oh….AHHHHH!"

Anna's soft whispers turned into screaming again and her eyes were wide open, just as Bodie and Amara disappeared. A puddle of wetness was now on the floor between Anna's legs, spreading out across the square tiles. Her water broke when she took the marble from Amara and gave it to her unborn son, gave it to Sam.

Art ran back into the room, nearly slipping on the blood on the floor. He crouched beside Anna, where Amara had been just a few seconds earlier.

"Okay, honey, okay," he said, putting one hand on her head to stroke her hair and taking the other hand, the one that had held Amara's hand with the marble in it. "Okay, I called the police and the ambulance. Your water's broken but you're okay. You're gonna be okay."

She settled down and looked at Art with a pained look on her face.

"My baby…"she whispered, putting her hand with his hand in it on her belly. "Our baby…our Sam…he's our Sam."

"Yes, honey, yes," Art said, nodding. "Yes, he's our

Sam...our Sam...our boy."

Sam has slumped against me and now he's crying.

"I'm their boy...I'm their boy," he says into my shoulder as I hug him.

I can hear the sounds of the sirens coming closer but then that sound changes and everything changes and we're back on the street corner, but still back then.

There I was, standing on the corner on the other side of the street. I looked pretty sad.

And there was Al, on the other side of the street, running towards the opposite corner from us. He was limping and he was having trouble breathing. He still had one of those painting knives in his hand. I look to my left and I can see the bus coming, behind the car that's just gone through the intersection. The bus will be here in a couple of seconds.

Al was slowing down as he came up to the corner but he looked confused. He sees me, back then across the street from him, but shakes his head and looks at the other corner, where me and Sam are standing right now. His eyes got wide and his face darkened and he got really mad.

"YOU!" he screamed, running into the street, raising his hand with the knife in the air. He sees me then and he sees me now but he doesn't care about that. It's Sam he somehow sees, even though we're just watchers from another time and we're not even really here, it's Sam he wants.

"YOU HAVE TO DIE! I'M GOING TO KILL—"

The bus plowed into him at full speed because the driver was looking in his rearview mirror and didn't see Al until the very last second. The bus driver's foot was in the air, between the gas and the brake, when there was that harsh thud of the bus hitting Al. The tires of the bus locked as the driver finally pushed down on the brakes, so Al was knocked ahead of the bus for a split second and then he fell to the street. The momentum of the bus carried it forward to Al and then over him, the front right tire went up and down over his body, as the whole bus shook and rattled before stopping.

Sam looks away and covers his eyes for the worst part of that but I didn't look away, then or now.

I feel a little better because I always thought it was me he saw and me he was running across the street to try and kill and that had always made me feel bad. But Sam doesn't feel better. He feels a lot worse for coming back here, for seeing this moment. For finding out that after his grandfather couldn't kill him when he was still in his mother's womb, he tried one last time to kill him on this street corner, his mind so far gone that he could see Sam in the future. Into our now.

But that lasted for like two seconds before the bus knocked him down and killed him.

The street changes but not too much and we're back in the right now but like then, nobody can see us but I can see Sam. He's looking down and his hand is still over his face. He's turning his head from side to side and his shoulders are shaking.

"How many more?" he cries. "How many more die because of me?"

That's a good question, I think to myself but don't say it as I hug him again. I guess that's up to you, Sam.

House call (Kathy)

I'm gonna be a lawyer when I grow up.

Or maybe I'll move to France.

I've been calling this Gilles Parenteau, Lily's lawyer, since midnight our time, 9 a.m. in Paris, and the phone just rings and rings. I call back every five minutes and it just rings. Nobody answers, no voice mail, nothing.

At 9:35 his time, a woman answers on the fifth ring.

"Oui? Allo? Bureau de Gilles Parenteau," she says quickly. She sounds young and efficient.

"Oh...right," I say, taken off guard that someone answered. My little speech in French that I had all ready has just disappeared so I just make do.

"Bonjour... uh... je m'appelle Kathy et...uh...je voudrais parlez...uh...avec Monsieur Parenteau,... uh... s'il vous plait," I manage to get out.

"Good morning, Kathy," she answers in perfect English. "M. Parenteau is meeting with a client at the moment. May I ask your business with M. Parenteau, please?"

Alex has long gone home but Mom is still up, all wired like me. We're still downstairs and she's on the other couch, sitting on the edge of the cushion, watching me. She's being supportive—she knows I can do this.

"Well, it's confidential and, sorry, I would rather talk to him directly, if I can," I tell her, not trying to sound like a bitch for hoping to blow past his assistant.

"Kathy, where are you calling from?" the assistant asks, catching me off-guard.

"Canada."

"Where in Canada?" she asks, a little chuckle in her throat. "It is the second largest country in the world."

"I'm calling from Kelowna, which is in the province of British Columbia," I say, expecting her to say "where the hell is that?" so I keep explaining. "It's not too far from Vancouver, where they had the Winter—"

"M. Parenteau has a client in Kelowna," she cuts me off. "Is this call in regards to Lily?"

"Yes, yes it is," I answer, a little startled.

"One moment, Kathy."

She abruptly puts me on hold and I'm listening to some guy yelling in opera. I hold the phone away from my ear.

"It was his assistant and she said—" I start telling Mom but then I hear a man's voice on the phone.

"Hello, Kathy from Kelowna," I hear him say but I don't get the phone to my ear until he's done saying Kelowna. "Are you there? This is Gilles Parenteau speaking."

His English is also perfect. I can't hear an accent at all. I bet he worked in Canada or maybe he's from Quebec or something. Maybe that's how Lily met him. His voice is warm and kind. I was expecting this abrupt and rude French guy.

"Good morning, sir," I say to him, being all formal. "I'm sorry to bother you."

"It is no bother, Kathy, and there is no need to apologize. It is very late in Kelowna so how I can help you?"

"Well, I have a letter from Lily and it says I should call you since you're her lawyer. I have a lot of questions that I was hoping you could answer," I say, doing my best polite voice. I want to jump into the phone and shout at him with every question I have about all of this.

"I have been expecting your call, Kathy, and I look forward to meeting you in person. My flight to Toronto leaves in three hours. From there, I will fly to Vancouver and then to Kelowna. I expect to be in your city this evening. Are you available for a meeting tonight, that is tonight in the Pacific time zone?"

What? He was expecting my call? How did he know?

Mom sees the confusion in my face and she mouths "What?" I answer him and her at the same time.

"Yes, I can meet you tonight."

Mom's eyes get wide and now she looks as confused as I feel.

"I have one other meeting before you in Kelowna, so I cannot give you a precise time but it will be later in the evening. I will call on you then. Go to sleep now and I will see you soon."

"Okay, but what about—"

There are two quick clicks and then nothing. He hung up on me.

I pull the phone away and click it off.

"He's coming here," I say, as much as to myself as to Mom. She's jumped up and is now sitting beside me.

"He'll be here tomorrow night," I tell her. Mom looks calm but I can tell she's nervous. "It was like he was expecting me to call him."

Mom sits up straight, nodding slowly.

"Maybe he was," she says, looking away as she thinks. "Her death made the news, since her accident was unusual."

Her death.

Sometimes it hits me that Lily is dead but now that I know more of what she was, I feel different about that. It's not like I'm not sad or anything, it's not like that. I miss her really bad but there's part of me that expects her to walk through the door any minute. I mean, how does someone live that long and then get killed by getting hit in the face with a baseball? Of all the stupid ways to go, that has to be the stupidest.

It's Sam's disappearance that's really eating me up inside because it's like I've lost two friends at the same time. And Sam isn't Lily. He's less mature and not as strong. I hope he hasn't done anything stupid. I hope I can still find him. I hope he wants to be found and will come home. I've already heard some people say maybe he jumped off the bridge into Okanagan Lake in the middle of the night but I don't believe it. The police don't believe it, either, or they say they don't anyway, because he didn't leave a note and because of Lily's letters. They think he might be in on it, somehow. That part I do believe but I just can't figure out how he fits into Lily's story.

"Kathryn?" Mom says in a voice that lets me know it's not the first time she's said my name but I've been thinking so hard that I didn't hear her the first time.

"Mmm? Yeah?" I answer.

She's on her feet and she's reaching out to me.

"C'mon, it's been quite a day and tomorrow will be—" she stifles a yawn. "—a big day, too."

I take her hand and stand up. She pulls me right into her arms and gives me a big hug. I smell her perfume and her hair spray just a tiny bit and then it's gone and I'm chasing it but I can't get it back. That's how I feel about Lily and Sam. I know once I talk to M. Parenteau that I'll know enough to figure this out and maybe find Sam.

Mom says good night and heads upstairs. I walk down the hall to my room but I don't go in. Instead, I turn and go into the spare room or what was Lily's room. I've been sleeping here a lot since she died and tonight won't be any different. My brain is spinning but I know I'll sleep. My eyes are heavy and I feel tired in my bones from everything that happened today. I'm so lazy that I just take my jeans off before getting under the covers.

The toughest part of today was not finding that stuff in the safety deposit box or the storage locker or talking to Mom and Alex about it. It was seeing Sam on the street and running after him and then he wasn't there. I was so sure that was him. I don't feel like crying again, though. I lie there and stare at the blue numbers of the clock, clenching my teeth and wondering if I'm going crazy a little.

I don't shut off the light.

Last visit (Sam)

Missy walks me the last few blocks from the corner of Cadder and Pandosy to my house. She holds my hand tight and gives it a few extra squeezes every couple of minutes to let me know...what? Everything will be alright? It'll all be over soon? There's more hurt to come? I don't know.

I do know one thing. Before, I would have blamed Missy for what happened to my grandpa but now I don't. It was Amara the whole time and I knew that, in my heart and in my head I knew that, but I kept thinking there had to be more. And there was. Bodie was in on it, too, and I knew that, too. He just had to be. I also know why I didn't do anything about it. I was so sure I could be better than what I was made to be, so sure I could control this power no one, not even a guardian, never mind another human, had ever had, that I blamed myself when things went wrong, when people and guardians died. And it is my fault and there are no excuses. Responsibility starts with me and I now understand that just being alive puts everyone at risk. I might not be able to hide somewhere on the other side of the universe.

All I did was stand on a street corner and I became responsible for the death of my grandfather and I wasn't even born yet. Yep, that's pretty messed up.

We stop in front of the house and I stare at it. So many memories, so many good times. I can't help but smile a little and relax. No matter what I am and what I've become, this is where I live. This is my home. I want to go running inside and see Mom and Dad but I know I can't. I get to see them one last time but they will never see me again. It kills me to think about the suffering they've gone through, they will go through, because of me.

No, they won't go through any more suffering because of me. All of this will end, somehow and soon. I'm not helpless here. I can make things happen and I have to keep looking for a way out, a way to fix things, a way to make it better. If I don't believe in that, I might as well just do what Amara made me to do and that's that. There has to be a choice somewhere and I just can't see it yet. I have to keep looking. I can't give up.

And I have to see the little things. Was it better for my grandfather to die the way he did, instead of suffer more, and make Mom and Dad suffer more, too? I can't say but maybe it was for the better. Maybe dying and death can be good, not all the time but once in a while, because it lets the living keep going. They were able to focus on being parents and raising me and Sara, instead of worrying about crazy Al in the psych ward. It's my mom and dad who made me like this, wanting to do the right thing for everyone. It's Amara and Bodie who put that darkness inside of me. It's part of me but it's not the most important part. It's not.

Missy is hugging me now and I'm crying because what else is there to do? I'm not sad for me but I'm so sad for my parents. They put all of their dreams into me and Sara and this is what they get—a dead daughter and a son who's disappeared from the face of the Earth.

Sara.

I figure one more little thing out, one more cruel jab that hit my parents. Amara must have come back, when I was little and Mom was pregnant with Sara. She must have cornered Mom somewhere alone and gave her that last little piece of Samael, that she just couldn't bear to part with the first time, with me. I don't have to go back and see it to know that happened. I can feel it.

"It's not fair," I say into Missy's shoulder, thinking about Mom and Dad and how much hurt they've had to take.

"Oh, Sam, it never is," she says back, rubbing the back of my head. "It never will be."

We stand there for another minute and then I move out of her arms. Missy looks down at her feet.

"So, we should go soon, okay?" she says, quietly.

"How come? We just got here," I answer. Now I'm suspicious. What's she up to?

"They're coming back from the store," she says, looking up at me, checking to see if I'm staying calm. "They'll be here in a minute."

"So? They can't see us." I'm looking up the block for the van to turn the corner. "And how do you know where they are?"

Missy just shakes her head.

"Because I've been with them since Lily died and you disappeared," she answers, scolding me a little. "I can be in more than one place at the same time, too, you know. I'm everywhere there's someone hurting. It's not all about you all the time. And with the way your mom is feeling right now, she might not see you but she might feel you here. That wouldn't be good."

The van is turning the corner onto our street. Missy steps forward and takes my hand.

"Follow me."

Instead of running behind a house or hiding behind that parked car across the street, Missy takes me up. And it's not this gradual up, like flying would feel like. We're on the street and then we're 100 feet in the air, directly over where we were standing a minute ago. It's how I disappeared when I felt Lily die. I didn't think about it. I just imagined myself in the furthest place from Earth I could and I was there. This is harder because I'm still human and it feels like I'm standing on air. I look down to see the van pulling into the driveway and it feels like I'm going to fall but Missy squeezes my hand to keep me steady.

Instead of going into the garage, Dad stops in the driveway. He gets out first and he's almost halfway around the van before Mom starts to get out. She's moving so slow and Dad is there to help her. His arm is around her and she leans into him, letting him guide her to the steps. I can't see Missy around her but I know she's there, around and right through Mom, like a cold fog. She's got a hold of Dad, too, but it's different. Dad still thinks I'm coming back. He hasn't lost hope like Mom has. He takes her inside but then he's back a minute later to take a few bags out of the back of the van.

I want to go down and talk to him but what would I say? What could I tell him that would make him understand? There's nothing I can do and nothing I can say. I have all of this power to destroy but I can't fix anything. I can't put them back together. I can't put myself back together.

But I know who can help me. Kathy pops into my head and I can hear her telling me something that'll make it make more sense. She'll give me something to hold onto. I look a few blocks over and I think I can make out the roof of her house. But Missy isn't moving and she isn't letting go of my hand.

"I don't think that's a good idea yet," she says, when I look at her. "I think you should talk to Cam about that. Let's go back to the lake."

"But I don't need Cameron's permission to go see Kathy," I answer. I'm not mad or anything and I don't raise my voice. I'm just pointing out the obvious.

"No, you don't, but I think you should talk to him first. I think he could help you with that," she smiles, trying to reassure me.

Her smile isn't natural and it doesn't look good on her. It just curls her face up but I know she's trying. It's her effort that makes me smile back. I'm about to answer but Missy has already taken us back to the beach. Cameron is standing on the grass next to a tree, since there is an old couple sitting together on the bench, not talking to each other but looking out together onto the water. They're holding hands.

Cameron walks over to me quickly, catching me off guard, since I just got my bearings. He must have been expecting us.

"This couple will be leaving shortly and then I want you to sit," he commands me. "I will be back soon."

He turns to leave but I grab his arm. Or try to. He slips right through and keeps moving away but I can hear him.

"Missy, come with me, please. Sam, wait."

I try to squeeze her hand to keep her with me but she's already gone.

"But—" I protest, stepping forward to follow.

Missy turns back, walking backwards away from me. "Wait, Sam, it'll be fine."

"But—"

She cuts me off.

"I think we're going to get her for you," she says, just before they both disappear.

What? They're going to get her? I can't let them do that. What if they—?

The old couple sitting on the bench get up together. Still holding hands, they start to walk towards downtown, not talking to each other, not needing to. They're in no rush and looking at them somehow calms me down. I go sit on the bench and let myself fully take shape. For the first time since Lily died, I am all in one place, all my physical self and the rest of me, too.

I wonder if this will be the last time I do it, too.

It feels good, the warm afternoon sun and the moist breeze from the lake tickling my skin. It makes it much easier not to run after Cam and Missy. I can trust them. They'll take care of Kathy and bring her here.

I take a deep breath and just soak it all in. I know what I saw earlier, how Amara put my darkness inside of me and how my grandfather died, but I can't change that and what does it change about now except that I know more? I know my parents are hurting really bad but I also realize that the best thing I can do for them now is to not hurt them anymore.

I put my hand on the crystal hanging around my neck that Crocodile gave me. I don't know what this is yet or what it means but I can wait.

I will wait.

Dressing up, hurrying up, waiting (Missy)

When I catch up to Cam, who's moving really fast for a guy who's supposed to be blind, he takes my hand and gives it a sharp squeeze. I don't understand why we just don't go to this girl's house. We're walking and I've done enough of that today with Sam.

"I wish you had not informed him of my plans," he says not very nicely.

"But, Cam—" I try to explain but he cuts me off.

"It makes no difference," he says, stopping fast and looking at me. "Have you taken on a physical shape before that is visible to humans?"

"No, why would I do that?" I answer, looking back at him nervous. "Wouldn't I just look the way I do now, except be visible enough so people can see me?"

"Yes, that is correct but don't do it yet. I will need you to do that with me soon," he says. "Our appearance needs to be appropriate for our upcoming meetings."

He is suddenly in a fancy suit that is so dark blue that it's almost black. It fits him really nice and he's got a sharp white shirt and a shiny red tie, too. His hair is combed neat to one side. He's got his usual thin white stick in his hand, that the blind people carry and he's got the thick sunglasses on because humans are so silly and the first thing they want to look at when they see a blind person is their eyes, like looking at them will explain why they're blind.

"How do you do that when you can't see like they do?" I ask him, because it's freaking me out a little and I really want to know.

"I have met enough well-dressed men that I simply used how they perceived themselves to shape my look. I trust it is fitting for the circumstances?" he asks.

"You look really handsome, Cam. Seriously," I tell him. "But what are the circumstances? You haven't told me that yet."

"Okay, Missy," and now he's talking nice and normal to me again but he's ignoring my question. "I want you to imagine yourself in the dress of the most beautiful woman you have seen in recent times."

I do but Cam just laughs, letting go of my hands and putting them against his chest but there's no holding in those laughs. He doesn't laugh very often but when he does, it just bubbles away like one of those bath things humans like to sit in that's really hot.

"Did I do something wrong?" I say, looking down. I don't have a mirror but I've got this really nice red shiny gown on, like the girls wear for their high school prom or the fancy movie star ladies wear to go to their awards nights. I even picked a red to match his tie. I'm thinking I look really pretty, maybe even beautiful. So why is he laughing at me? I don't like that.

"I am sorry for not making my instructions more precise, Missy," he manages to say but he's still chuckling. "You look extraordinary, my dear, but it is not what I seek."

"I do look nice, right?" I say, just to hear him say it again. I look "extraordinary." That's cool.

"Scintillating, my darling. But what I really need is for you to dress the way a beautiful woman who works in an office, in a position of power, dresses," he says.

I wish I could see into his head but I can only do that with people and guardians who are feeling really bad and hurting inside about stuff. So I think about this one lady I know who is a big boss at some big company but her husband is cheating on her and her son is in and out of addiction treatment places and always stealing from her. She's pretty miserable but she looks great, in her expensive jacket and blouse, with a nice skirt and pretty shoes. I attach those clothes to my appearance and hope that's more what Cam wants me to look like.

"Excellent," Cam says and I can tell he's happy. "A perfect choice, Missy."

I give him a nice big smile because he's giving me one.

"I'm glad you like it. Now what?"

"Now I feel like celebrating," he says, spreading his arms wide. "Let's go out as humans and have a fancy human meal."

"Sure," I smile back because that could be pretty fun. "But I hope you're paying because I don't have any money."

Cam laughs again.

"I have a sufficient form of payment to satisfy our needs in the human world. Shall we go?"

"I'm ready," I tell him.

Cam curls his hand and presses it lightly against his stomach while sticking his elbow out. I walk forward and put my hand on his arm, underneath the elbow, all formal like the people do when they dress up and go out. This is going to be so much fun.

He moves his head slightly, as if he's listening for something, then smiles and nods.

"Let's make ourselves visible to them now, Missy, while no one is looking. Just imagine yourself like you did with your clothing but as flesh and bone and blood as they are," he tells me.

I don't take his advice.

I just watch him do it and then imitate him. It's easier.

"There, we're now visible to all humans as humans ourselves, so no taking off," he says to me. "You're here in this one place with me and only here until later, alright Missy?"

I don't feel any different and I didn't feel a thing when we changed, whatever we did, so I just nod back.

"Sure, Cam. But what are these circumstances to dress like this and why are we going out for dinner? What about Sam? He's waiting for us to get his friend."

"He will wait because he has to and while he waits I hope he will finally understand what he needs to do, what he needs to become. Then we'll bring his friend to him."

I listen and I nod but I don't really understand. That's okay, though. I trust in Cam, just like always.

We walk out of the park together but Cam is so clever. He makes it look like I'm guiding him but he's the one leading me. He holds his white stick but doesn't use it because I'm here for appearances. He takes me to a fancy restaurant named Ric's Grill, right across the street from the park, and we get seated. I just trust Cam with every-thing—he orders an expensive red wine and two yummy steak dinners.

And we chat.

Everything has been about Sam and Lily and Amara and Bodie and stuff, so now it's back to the way it used to be. We tell stories about people we've met and other guardians we've bumped into from time to time and what they were like. All the stories are funny or at least really interesting, where we shake our heads and I say "wow" and Cam says "that is unusual, to say the least." We eat and that's pretty neat because it's a new thing for me and the food is pretty tasty. We have some chocolate cake thing with a red sauce on top for desert and it's even yummier.

"We should have just had this for dinner," I tell him, pointing at the cake with my fork.

He just laughs.

After coffee, we head out onto the sidewalk. It's dark outside now but the street lights are bright. We stand there for a minute and I'm about to ask him again what's going on. He keeps distracting me and then I forget.

"There is a taxi coming towards us to our left, I believe," he says. "Hold your hand up and it will pick us up."

I do as I'm told and just like he said, the yellow car pulls to a stop in front of us. The driver runs out really fast to help Cam and me, as if Cam is helpless or something, but Cam says thanks and so do I after we get into the back of the car and the driver shuts the door for us.

"Where to, folks?" he says cheerfully when he jumps back into his seat.

Cam says a number and a name, which I guess is an address to where we're going but it doesn't mean anything to me, and the driver starts us moving. I don't know what to say now that there's a person with us and Cam isn't talking now, either. He's looking out his window and I can tell his mood is changing. He's turning into serious Cameron again. I wonder if we're on our way to do something I won't like.

"When are we going to pick up Kathy?" I ask him, trying to be quiet but still sound nice.

"Hmm?" he says, turning back to me. "Oh, not until tomorrow morning. Well, it was supposed to be tomorrow night but things have changed. Events are moving faster than I had anticipated. We have another meeting tonight."

"Is that where we're going now?" I ask.

"That is correct," he answers, turning back to the window.

I want to ask who we're meeting but I can tell he's back thinking again so I sit back and turn to look out my own window. We pass the corner where I was with Sam earlier, when he saw his grandfather.

And then I start to feel them. There are guardians really close by.

The further we drive, the more I can feel them and not one or two but lots of them. We're getting closer and closer to them. I haven't felt so many guardians so close to me since…since…oh, no. Not this place.

I reach out and grab Cam's hand. He takes it and squeezes back but doesn't look at me. The driver is slowing down.

"The third driveway to your right, please," Cam says, leaning forward and holding out some money. "Just drop us off there. There is no need to go down. We can walk. And, please, keep the change."

"Sure thing," the driver says as he smoothly stops the car. He takes Cam's money. "Thank you, sir. You have a good night now."

"And you as well," Cam says as he starts to get out of the car.

I get out to and go over to him, taking his hand again. I am staying in a solid human form and in my nice clothes, just like he told me but I'm very nervous.

"Sshhh, my dear," he squeezes my hand. "We are in no danger."

The taxi turns around and zips past us, heading back towards the centre of Kelowna. We just stand in front of the driveway and everybody is here and looking at us. There are guardians everywhere, all of them in physical shape but not to humans. The driver didn't see any of them.

There's so many I've only met once or twice before. We're all here. I'm looking at all of them and they're looking at me. I smile at Camille, standing right in the front, but then Devi, standing beside her, has to ruin everything and start talking.

"Welcome, Cameron and Missy. You are the last two to arrive to this meeting," she says, glaring at both of us, going back and forth between me and Cam.

Beside her, Amara looks so happy. I could like her if she was always like this but she's never been like this.

Until now.

And Camille is practically dancing, she's so excited, and she's got an even bigger smile than Amara.

"Yay! Everyone's here! Let's get crackin'!" she shouts and there is a shiver that runs through all of the guardians behind her.

"Good evening, Devi," Cam answers. "Thank you for being so gracious as to have all of us here."

She nods.

"And greetings to you, Camille, my sister," he says to the little girl.

She dashes forward and gives Cam a big hug. He puts his free hand around her back, smiling.

"It's about time you got here," she says, stepping back and grinning. "Everything's ready to go."

Devi turns and holds out her hand, motioning for us to start walking down the driveway. The guardians start moving, heading towards the house and the lake. Camille has taken Cam's other free hand.

Here we are the three of us. Cameron and Camille and me but I always feel like I'm the odd one when we're together because their names sound almost the same and mine is different. But I don't feel this way very much because the three of us aren't in the same place very often.

And I always forget that I have a special relationship with both of them but they also have a relationship with each other.

I wonder what they talk about when it's just the two of them.

I don't get any time to think about that because Amara and Devi start walking behind us and I get nervous again.

"Everything's ready for what?" I lean towards Cam and whisper. "What is Camille talking about?"

He turns back to me. He's really calm and quiet.

"Missy," he says, gently. "This is how it ends."

Last night (Amara)

We all walk down together to the water after Missy and Cameron arrive. I even tolerate the fact that they are in full human form. Nothing can shatter my joy.

There is silence except for the stirring of the water and a light breeze. It feels as perfect as it should. We are looking at each other, quietly and respectfully.

And then Missy somehow finds a way to ruin it. It is her nature.

"What do you mean 'this is how it ends?' What is this all about? Why is everyone here? I don't like this." She is holding Cameron's sleeve and she does appear to be deeply concerned.

"I have brought all of you here because of Sam," Devi answers truthfully.

I had little to do with this. This is all her doing. This is Devi's nature—to control, even at this point. I wonder if she is making a mistake but I know better than to suggest any form of doubt to her.

"Sam is on the cusp of his evolution and I would like all of us to go together," Devi states. "Let us go to him now and let him begin the final destruction for which he was created."

"Cam, I don't like this, let's go. Why do we have to listen to her?" Missy says.

Devi just looks at her and she stops talking. Now she's like all of the other guardians, quiet and under her control. They all thought the same thing and Devi did that to them, too.

"I have come as you asked, Devi," Cameron says. "I would appreciate if you would not abuse Missy or any of the others."

"She is not being harmed," Devi answers. "I am merely asserting my control over her."

"You are taking your revenge upon her for what happened while Sam was in mourning and she was fulfilling her duty," Cameron says, walking up to her.

That explains why Devi was not able to control Missy when we wished to speak to Sam. I had been curious why but now I understand. Sam's agony at the death of Lily made Missy invulnerable for that short time, that even Devi could not control her. Now that Sam is out of Missy's grasp, Devi can do as she wishes. She has not taken control of me yet but I suspect she would the moment my interests no longer matched hers. That is of no concern to me because I know she will have no effect on Sam.

But now this is interesting. Cameron is not one to assert himself in this manner, challenging Devi like this. Is his power enough to stop her? It does not matter. I need to intervene and deal with my agenda. I step between them, my hands out to both of them.

"My friends, this is not a time to quarrel," I say. "Cameron, Devi is only fulfilling her duty by taking control of this situation. Please respect her nature."

Cameron turns to me but I have forgotten until now that I am completely blind to him. He has to concentrate just to hear my voice.

"Amara?"

He lets go of Missy and holds his hand out in my direction. I take it.

"Yes, Amara, yes," he finally speaks. "I came because Devi called but I see now it is you who really wishes to speak."

"Are you bringing the human girl to him?" I ask, trying not to show my impatience.

"Of course," he answers. "He will be saying his goodbyes and she will be the last. He may not yet realize it but I suspect he will soon enough."

"And then he will finish it." I say, looking away, out across the water towards where I know Sam sits and waits.

I feel this incredible sense of relief. I have waited so long and worked so hard for this time to finally be here. Lily stopped me before but there is no one, nothing, that can stop Sam from fulfilling his role. This entire existence has been wrong and now it will be made right again.

"You state it as if it is a foregone conclusion," Cameron says, laughing quietly. "When will you learn? When will both of you learn? He sets the timetable, not you or me or Devi or anyone else."

"When I bring all of us to him, he will have no choice," Devi purrs like a cat.

Cameron turns to her slowly.

"Take me and take Amara under your control," he says, smiling. "Take us to him as your offering. He will not spare you, Devi, because there is one of us you do not have the power to control and never will."

"Camille will fulfill her function and nothing more," Devi answers, shaking her head. "If there is one guardian Sam would like to eliminate more than any of us, it is her."

Before Cameron can answer, Camille speaks, letting go of Cameron's hand and turning to stand in front of us.

"I don't like what any of you are saying," she shouts. Cameron lets go of my hand.

"Especially you," she says, pointing at Devi, who stands her ground but I can tell she was not expecting to hear that. "You have control but you can stop them from doing things, like talking or running away," she adds, shaking her head. "You can't make them do what you want. It doesn't work like that."

Devi looks away and I understand the limitation of her power. My sense of purpose has made me susceptible to her power. Camille's sense of purpose knows no limits so Devi's power is meaningless to her.

"And you," she now points at Cameron, who seems to have no problem hearing or seeing her. He recoils slightly and is facing her directly. "You talk about me as if you know me. You don't know anything about me and never will. Just because I tell you things doesn't mean you know me, you know."

"Same with you," she says, now looking at me and crossing her arms. "I'm friends with Sam and he's friends with me. It's got nothing to do with any of you."

"I made him for you," I say back to her, refusing to back down.

"Liar, liar, pants on fire" she says, shaking her head. "You made him for you."

"But he gave you his heart," I insist. "It was beating and living and you took it from him when he offered it. He lives for you."

"And when Sam asks me for it, I'll give it back," she says, bobbing her head in defiance.

Now it is my turn to be startled. Suddenly I see a massive gap in my plan. If she gives him back his beating heart, then could he become human once more? No. That can't happen. That must not happen. That is not what is supposed to happen. I look at Devi and Cameron, who stand to my left. They are thinking the same thing. Devi glances at me and then looks back at Camille.

"So why are you here?" Devi asks but in a calmer voice. She is respectful to Camille. I believe we all are.

"I'm never too far from my pal Sam," she shrugs her shoulders. "Not anymore. I think he's about to do something really, really big."

"You do not know the outcome, Camille?" I ask quietly.

"Not even Mr. Bodie knew that and he knew everything," she says, sticking out her bottom lip and shaking her head.

Then she stops and looks up, her brow twisted in thought.

"No, wait. There was that one thing I didn't tell him but I told Cameron that, about what I felt when Lily died," she says. "I think there's something else out there, maybe another one of us that we didn't know about and Sam didn't know that, either, but I think he's about to find out."

"What?" Devi shouts. "What are you talking about? There is a guardian Bodie didn't know about? That is ridiculous! You speak nonsense!"

Camille's stare at Devi not only freezes her but the rest of us as well. When Camille finally speaks, it feels like every word shakes the ground under my feet.

"Who said he was a guardian? He's not a guardian, not like you and me. He's way bigger. He doesn't have just little one piece of the puzzle, like we do. He's got them all, you know."

There is a movement around us. For a moment, everything starts to dissipate and then it comes together again. It is gone as quickly as it came but now there is a presence among us but it is everywhere, not just in one place. I can feel it surround us but it is not tangible.

"Sam," Cameron speaks softly. "He is here with us."

Camille's face opens in a large smile. She looks up into the sky, turning her head in several directions. She's admiring something I am unable to see.

"Won't be long now, guys," she says, turning and starting to walk away.

"Until what?" Cameron calls.

"Until he finds what he's looking for, silly, or should I say until he finds who he's looking for," she calls back, waving her hand behind her head. "You and my nice sister I like should go get Sam's friend like you said you would."

The darkness takes her and she is gone.

I stand still with my eyes closed, trying to let Sam's presence soak into me but it is apart from me. I cannot bring it into me and I am no closer to it no matter what direction I turn or move.

"Amara," Cameron says, putting his hand on my arm. His voice is sympathetic.

"Leave me," I say, pulling my arm away without

looking at him. "Go do as you were told."

"I shall," he answers.

Cameron takes Missy's hand and starts to walk away, following Camille into the dark. Missy is still in Devi's grasp but the further Cameron takes Missy, the less Devi's hold on her remains. I watch Devi gritting her teeth, trying to stop him from taking Missy from her but she is unable to prevent it.

"I forgive you, Devi," he calls from the darkness and his words strike her like vicious blows, knocking her down. Her control of all of the others is released.

Before Devi can recover herself, they are on her, all of the other guardians, and she is powerless to stop them. They will not forgive her. She is screaming because they have her and they are hurting her now, pulling away her essence of control in rough, jagged pieces.

Camille comes running back up the beach and picks up the thick iron chain left lying in the sand. All of us are watching her. She pulls the chain tight and then turns in a slow circle, looking at all of the guardians gathered in her presence. Her nostrils flare and her eyes are wild.

"He forgave her and you should have forgiven her, too," she yells at them.

None of them challenge her and they leave quickly, scattering without a word.

She turns and walks up to me.

"You were nice to her," she says to me. "Will you keep her with you until it's, you know, it's time?"

"Yes," I whisper. "I will keep Devi with me."

"Bend your head down, okay?" she says, lifting both ends of the chain up towards my neck.

I go down on one knee and bow my head.

She fastens the chain to my neck and it transforms

into a thin, gold necklace but I can feel the weight of Devi's essence, all of that control. I can barely move my head but I manage to stand up.

Camille steps back, nods and smiles at me.

"I know that's a lot to carry and everything but you look nice."

I smile weakly back at her.

Looking back, looking forward, with hope (Max)

I can barely recall my previous life, the one I had before I was left in charge of holding everything together, of keeping the system going. I don't remember my friends or my parents except that I am certain I had both at some time. The first thing I distinctly remember was discovering the maintenance man before me. I was frightened but I was also certain of what I had to do and I did it without hesitation.

I have no memory of being distracted by guardians and self-doubt like Sam. Perhaps I shouldn't be so hard on him because maybe I hesitated when it was my time. Maybe there were others holding me back, too. Maybe I was in love like he was. Maybe I lost people I loved. Maybe I killed people I loved.

If I did, I do not remember.

This has been my reality now for so long, being the maintenance man.

As this existence winds down, I look forward to my own peace but I do so with some guilt because Sam will pay for my peace, in the same way I paid for the salvation of my predecessor. The more I look at him, the more I realize how silly I was to have faith in a guardian as weak and shallow as Samael. The best creature for the task had to be someone who lived and at least faced the prospect of his own mortality, someone with choice and doubt and youth and belief. I wonder if I was like that, too.

I wish I could remember. I hope I was like him. I hope he is like me.

I hope he finds me and I hope he comes here. I want to meet him and talk to him.

And when he gets here...

I look out over the table, at all of the gears and pulleys and machinery that hold existence together, that keep me going, that make life live.

I hope he smashes the shit out of it.

Bodie's ninth question (Sam)

Are you willing to be right in front of her and completely out of sight?

I'm not sure who her is anymore with this question. I always thought it was about Lily but now that I'm sitting here on the park bench, looking out at Okanagan Lake, watching the sun go down, I'm wondering if Bodie meant Kathy.

That's who I'm waiting for and I have to trust Missy and Cameron on this. Well, I don't have to but I will. Missy has caused me all sorts of hurt but she hasn't lied to me or tried to kill me or anyone else.

So is that the test?

They're going to bring Kathy here and I'm supposed to just sit here, invisible to her but right in front of her? Forget that. I've made myself visible, I've brought myself back in my own skin and I'm going to stay there, so she can see me.

No, Bodie's question is about Lily because the questions before were about her, too.

And now I remember the present that Crocodile gave me. I unclasp it from my neck so I can look at the crystal more closely. It's not Lily but it's supposed to represent her. That's what I told Missy. It's a reminder of my connection to her and that connection hasn't disappeared because Lily is dead. It lives as long as I do.

But it's more than that. It's a key to a door I need to go through. I see that now. I let myself soak up all the want inside of the crystal, letting it fill me and it's like I'm with her again, the two of us together. I can't see her but I can feel her all around me and I can feel myself all around her.

I feel myself drifting backwards in time, towards her, and her life, and I experience that again, being in front of her and completely out of sight. I can share those experiences with her but she doesn't know I'm there. But it feels wrong. Her path is set and I know what the outcome is. I know she has to kill Samael, has to kill those other people or we don't come to this moment when we meet, when we connect, everything leading up to here. We would come to a different moment and this moment, me sitting here on a bench in City Park in the dark, wouldn't exist or it wouldn't be the same even if it did.

As I come back into the present, I feel them, Cameron and Missy, and then I feel all of them. There's Crocodile, looking up, seeing me. All the guardians are at Amara's place on the lake south of the city, where I first went after her to get her to leave Lily and me alone.

Where I killed two guardians, Cherry and Ruby.

Where I betrayed Lily but she saved me.

Where I gave my beating heart to Crocodile.

Something's happening there and I jump to my feet,

ready to go, but then I stop. They told me to wait so I sit back down. It's not like there's any big threat. They're just there. But what are they waiting for?

I don't like this. This is exactly the kind of crap that got me into trouble before. Amara is definitely there and so is Devi. What are those two up to now?

And that reaction is exactly what got me into trouble before, too. I don't have to react to them all going there. I can let them just hang out there and I'll hang out here, waiting for Missy and Cameron to come back with Kathy.

I can sit here and think about this crystal in my hand, feel how it brings me to Lily. I put it back around my neck.

I can sit here and think about my question from Bodie.

I can just sit here.

Just sit.

The park gets dark and quiet as it gets late and now I'm alone, although I guess I was alone before since I'm not human anymore, anyway, and I'm not a guardian, either. I'm by myself not just where I am but who I am.

And I lean back into the bench, relaxing, my arms spread out to each side of me on the top of the back rest. The only word I can use to describe how I feel and what I'm doing at the same time is a word Pete liked using but it always sounded stupid, like I was trying too hard, when I said it. I'm chilling. Just chilling. Just hanging out, all mellow.

That doesn't begin to describe it.

As the night goes on, I begin to drift, not to sleep but it's the closest thing I've had to sleep since that day on the beach, when I gave up my heart and lost my human self. I feel myself, still sitting on the bench by the water, spreading out over the city, then over the continent, then over the world, and then past that.

I chuckle to myself, back on the bench, that I wonder if this is what it's like on LSD or one of those old school drugs that make you have hallucinations. I'm one with the universe, man. Trippy.

It feels like I'm everywhere and nowhere at the same time. I'm with Lily and she's with me but I'm past that. I can feel the bright sun and the heat of the desert on the other side of the world but I can also feel, at the same time, the heat of the Earth's molten core because I'm there, too. And I can feel every massive explosion on the Sun's surface and every burning rock on the surface of Mercury and every frozen rock on poor distant Pluto, not even considered a real planet anymore.

And beyond that, I feel the light and the life and the energy of distant solar systems and then distant galaxies, surrounded by the huge darkness of space and time. And then I fall back into time, too, watching it all rewind. I've done this before, watching Lily's life backwards and forwards, but never experiencing it on such a huge scale. I see the whole universe as one place and one time and then I even feel past that, to the other universes and the other times. I can't see it, I don't even know how I would explain it to someone, but I know it's there and I know there are places beyond this universe, beyond this experience, where I could go and never be found by the guardians of this place.

Except there are guardians in those places, too. In all of them.

But there is only one me.

Unless...

And then the truth comes to me. I don't need to know everything like Bodie. I just need to know this one thing.

I just need to do this one thing. And that thing is starting to take shape inside me

And I see now where I'm supposed to go and who I'm supposed to talk to about that.

There's someone I couldn't see before. Like Cameron, he was hidden from me until I was ready to look in his direction. But now that I've seen all the places, I can hear what's holding everything together and now I can see who's making all of that happen.

He's not God or anything like that. He's just a guy, maybe like the Wizard of Oz or something, the guy behind the scenes and he's not far.

He's waiting for me. He's been waiting for a while.

Maybe he's got some answers for me. I want to go see him right away.

But now I'm really out of time.

All the distance I've crossed, all the time I've crossed, and now I have to return to the bench and the moment.

It's early morning. The sun is up in Kelowna but the park is still quiet. There are three footsteps on the path, coming towards me, all human but two of them are just in human form and visible to humans, not really human.

It's Cameron and Missy.

And then I see Kathy with them and I pull all of me back into this place and this time.

And then she sees me.

The visit (Kathy)

Like I can sleep. I mean really.

I lie in my clothes on top of the bed, leaving the light on, and let my mind wander, going over everything that happened today—the bank, the storage locker, talking with Mom, talking with Alex, talking with M. Parenteau.

And then I start thinking of everything that's happened in the last couple of weeks. Lily gets killed when a baseball smashes into her face. Sam disappears. We can't find Lily's dad or anyone who even knows her before she came to Kelowna. I find Lily's laptop and the letters. The cops show up the day before the funeral, asking about those letters she sent to those four families, wanting an explanation for how she knew about those murders.

It's hard to breathe, never mind to cry, when I think of all of that and the weight of it just sits on my chest like some big sumo wrestler.

Somehow, somewhere in there, my eyes must have closed, because the next time I look at the clock it's 4:37. I groan as I sit up. That sumo wrestler used me as a training bag while I was sleeping. I go down the hall to the bathroom, turn on the light but don't look in the mirror because I'm sure I look like shit. I strip and jump into the shower, making it as hot as I can take it. I can feel my muscles loosening and relaxing. I catch myself sighing more than once. I start to feel like myself again or at least a version of myself that I recognize in the mirror.

I let my routine take over—getting dressed, doing my hair, slapping on a face. It's comfortable, going through those daily motions, like everything's normal and this is just another normal day, except that I haven't had one of those for a while but at least I can feel normal, maybe for a few minutes while putting myself together.

I actually don't look that bad, considering how little sleep I got and how little sleep I've been getting. I've found some answers that don't really make sense about Lily but they explain a lot and I'm going to get more of an explanation tonight from a French lawyer flying halfway around the world to see me.

But he's got another meeting first. I wonder what that could be. Could it have something to do with Sam? I know he's not dead—I don't know how I know but I know it—and I know he's tied up in this thing with Lily. But she's dead, at least as far as I know, but I can't get ahead of myself. Deep breath. No need to guess because the lawyer is coming and hopefully he's got lots of answers.

I'm tempted to start going through Lily's stuff that we brought home from the locker but I hold off. I'll have all day to go through it. I'm going to check online about some of the coins and the paintings and stuff because I'm sure it's all worth lots of money but I'm more interested in the history and maybe it'll give me some clues of where Lily and Cindy were before and where they came from. It'll be a history project I can actually be interested in.

I'm thirsty so I go upstairs and quietly go into the kitchen. It's light out now but the sun's not fully up over the mountains. I pour a glass of orange juice and drink the whole thing in one shot. I'm standing at the counter, thinking about whether I should have toast or just a bowl of cereal, when I hear a car door shut outside. I walk to the front window and look out.

There's a shiny black car right in front of the house. It's not a limo but it's one of those nice big cars, with the tinted windows, that's used to drive important people around. There's a young guy in a black suit, a white shirt and a skinny black tie standing by the passenger doors, facing the house. I move back, startled, because he sees me at the same time I see him.

I creep up to the window, staying behind the curtain and look out again. The young guy is still there and I'm sure he sees me but I don't care because it's the two people coming up the walk to our front door that I'm interested in. It's a well-dressed guy in a suit and a younger girl, also dressed nice.

As quickly as I can without making too much noise, I race out of the living room and down the hall to meet them at the door. I don't want them to ring the doorbell or even knock and wake everyone up. This must be the lawyer from Paris but how did he get here so fast and what's he doing here at 6 in the morning? I don't have time to think about it.

I open the front door and step out onto the mat, quietly closing the door behind me. The man and the young girl, she looks about the same age as me, stop on the top step.

"Please accept my sincerest apologies for showing up at this hour, Kathy. It was not our intent to startle or inconvenience you," the man in the suit says. He is wearing thick sunglasses and has a white cane in his hand. I barely hear what he's saying as I figure out, because I'm such a freaking genius, that he's blind. "I am Gilles Parenteau but my English friends call me Cameron."

He pauses for a second, as if he's not quite sure what he should say but then he continues talking. He sounds like he's in a little bit of a rush.

"This is my associate, Missy, and I—"

Missy cuts him off.

"I'm really sorry we came to you like this," she says, sticking out her hand to shake mine. "We need you to come with us right away, so we can meet Sam."

Cameron turns sideways at Missy but he's not mad or even surprised. He feels for Missy's arm, which is still out in front of me waiting for my handshake, and pulls it back. He starts to apologize but I cut him off.

"What is going on here? How did you guys get here so fast? What do you know about Sam? Have you taken him?" The more I talk, the louder my voice is getting and the more scared I'm getting. I don't even get to my next question, which is "Are you here to take me away, too?" I step back and, still facing them, put my hand on the doorknob.

"Kathy, please, we mean no harm," Cameron says, his hands up in front of him, trying to be peaceful.

Missy is more direct. She steps up onto the top step with me and her eyes, on the same level as mine, focus hard on me.

"Kathy, me and Cam are people like Lily was and like Cindy was and like Bodie was, we're not like you but…" she leans forward and whispers, "…the driver guy is human like you but he doesn't know about me and Cam so let's keep it that way."

She leans back and just keeps talking low, never taking her eyes off me.

"You've been so sad and so angry for the last couple of weeks after Lily died and Sam took off but he needs to talk to you now and alone, not with your mom there and not with his parents. He's already said his goodbyes to them."

"Goodbye?" I whisper.

"Kathy, Sam's more like us now. He looks fine on the outside but he's become something else and so he needs to go and there are things he needs to do. I don't know what those things are but maybe he'll tell you. He's sitting on a bench in City Park right now, waiting for you. We're friends of his and we can answer a few of your questions on the drive over."

She smiles at me and then puts out her hand but not

for a handshake. She wants to hold my hand and guide me. She inches forward.

"Trust me, Pumpkin," she says, using the name only my mom and Sam use. "I was a friend of Lily's and, even though he's been mean to me sometimes, I'm Sam's friend, too."

I stare back at her. She seems so familiar to me but I know I've never seen her before. She reminds me a lot of Lily. She's just as straightforward and to the point as Lily but she does it more simply. I believe every word she said and I know I can trust her.

There's also something about Cameron that pulls me to him, like I was attracted to Lily's dad, Bodie. With Cameron, there's just a feeling of safety. It's not that I didn't believe what he said, it's that I didn't like how he said it. He made a logical case for me to come with him but Missy talked to me, understood me.

"Go inside and leave a note for your mother so she does not worry," Cameron says. "Bring your cell phone and then come with us, please."

I reach forward and take Missy's hand, squeezing it.

"Okay," I tell her, smiling. "I'll be right back."

The instant I shut the door behind me, the smile falls off my face and I slip on a pair of shoes. I grab my cell off the counter and I quietly slip out the back door from the kitchen. I quickly go down the steps and run across the grass to the storage shed. I need to stand on my tippy-toes to reach the key on the door sill but I manage to grab it and unlock the shed. Haven't ridden my bike since last fall but it's leaning against the wall, just past the Halloween and Christmas decorations. I wiggle it out the door and onto the grass, close the door and just put the key in my pocket. The tires are a little soft but they're not flat enough to slow me down too much. The gate is a little bit tricky because we don't open it very often but I manage to do it without making much noise. It's so quiet out that every sound seems to boom in my ears.

I pull the gate so that it's up against the fence, rather than closing it, and then I'm on my bike, heading down the back alley. I'll be able to connect with Glenwood Avenue and then across Richter to Pandosy. If I ride hard, I can be to City Park in 10 minutes. I'm sure Cameron and Missy won't wait that long before they start knocking on the door but Mom can deal with them.

I'm out onto the pavement now, instead of the bumpy compacted gravel of the back alley and now I can really pick up speed. There's not much traffic yet so I'm able to cross Richter without having to stop.

I do trust Cameron and Missy to tell me what's going on but I don't want to hear it from them. I need to hear it from Sam, plus this is a good test to see if they are telling me the truth. If Sam really is waiting in City Park, then I really can trust them.

But what am I expecting Sam to say? And is that true that he's somehow become one of them? That would explain a lot, I guess. He wouldn't start looking older so we'd all figure that out pretty quick. But there's got to be more to it than that. I push as much of that out of my head as possible and concentrate on pedaling. It's flat all the way, thank God, but I push myself to go faster. The chain creaks and complains because it needs to be oiled.

Instead of waiting at the red light at Harvey, I jump the bike onto the sidewalk and head towards Abbott. This is a risky crossing because some of those people coming off the bridge come flying around that corner but I hit the break in traffic perfect and manage to cross Harvey without even slowing down. I ride on the sidewalk running along the entrance to the park, pedaling as hard as I can.

Just two blocks to go.

I'm sweating now and my heart is pounding but not just because of the effort. I'm close to getting some answers, I'm close to seeing Sam again. I just have to reach the end of Abbott, where it meets Bernard, and take a hard left onto the brick path that runs along the lake into the park. I know exactly which benches they mean.

"Aw, shit," I mutter, stopping pedaling and just gliding now, not sure what to do next.

A black car appears from Bernard Avenue and pulls up to the corner where I'll be making the turn into the park. Missy gets out of the car and waves at me while Cameron gets out more slowly and unfolds his white walking stick . He turns in my general direction, a small smile on his face.

I could ride across the grass, avoiding them. I glance over. There's someone sitting with his back to me on the third bench in, facing the water. I can't tell if it's him because he's in the shadows from the trees but there's definitely someone there. I look back just in time and have to swerve to avoid riding into a newspaper box. I nearly lose my balance but I manage to straighten out, the handlebars vibrating in my hands.

It doesn't matter now and I squeeze the brakes. I'm at the corner and Missy and Cameron are here. I try to look up the path but the way it curls along the lake, with the trees in the way, I can't see, so I look at them as the bike comes to a stop and I climb off.

"Do you wanna keep your bike and ride it home or do you want this guy to bring it back to your house in the trunk of his car?" Missy says, walking up to me.

I glare at her, too mad at myself for being so easily fooled.

"Aw, come on, Kathy," she continues, shrugging her shoulders. "We would have given you a ride if you wanted to come with us but the most important thing was to get you down here. And you saw him, right? That's why you almost rode right into that newspaper box."

She's smiling at me again but I don't care about her. I'm here for Sam. She said that's him. She takes the bike from me and walks over to the driver guy, motioning for him to pop open the trunk. I look at the path but just as the thought of making a run for it to Sam by myself pops into my head, Cameron has stepped forward, blocking my way.

"Please take my arm and guide me, Kathy," he says, looking slightly to the left of me. "I would like to ask you something."

He is holding out his left arm and, without thinking, I move to his side and grip his arm. We turn towards the path and start walking slowly, his white cane tapping in front of us. Missy quickly catches up and walks beside me. But something doesn't feel right. The path isn't smooth and there are bricks that have heaved and sagged over the years yet he's walking without stumbling. I look down and notice he's lifting his feet carefully as he walks. One step. Next step.

I glance at his face and he answers the question for me.

"I am blind to the light you use to see, Kathy, if that helps explain my situation," he says, still facing straight ahead, the cane tapping a beat to his words. "But that just leads to more questions, doesn't it? There are other ways to perceive the universe and its living inhabitants, Kathy, other senses I rely on. And that response leads to more questions."

The path is gently turning to the left, following the slight bend in the lake. I'm looking ahead because I should be able to see Sam in a minute. I'm interested in what Cameron is telling me but not as interested as he thinks I am. Then he cuts through that.

"I answered your question to segue into my question for you. How do you feel knowing beings like us exist and Lily was one of them?"

I don't have to think for a second for an answer. It's been sitting on my chest since I found Lily's letters and then the laptop and then it grew yesterday, looking in the safety deposit box at the bank, going through Lily's things at the storage locker, and it's still growing, walking here with Missy and Cameron.

"I feel small," I say, my voice sounding really far away in my ears. "And I feel like I'm getting smaller and smaller."

Missy pats my shoulder.

"Now you know how we feel around Sam," she says.

And there he is. He's looking out over the lake and I can tell he's thinking really hard about something but he looks pretty calm and relaxed, sitting there, leaning into the bench with his arms out across its back.

I feel everything at once. I'm so grateful he's alive. I want to hug him and then strangle him for making his mom and dad worry, making me worry, leaving me to have to go through all this stuff with Lily by myself. And I'm worried. He's become like them, they said, and now Missy says they feel small around Sam. He's new to them, too, and maybe he's more than them, somehow.

And then he turns and sees us.

I left go of Cameron's arm and I'm running to him.

Disappear (Sam)

I stand up as Kathy runs to me, a big smile on my face. I'm so happy to see her. She's the only real person, the only human, who might understand all of this with Lily and the guardians. Well, I'm sure she'll understand it about as much as I do, which I guess means she won't understand much of it at all.

It is what it is, as Pete used to say.

I've known Kathy for so long and I feel such a strong loyalty to her. Whatever I have to do next -- and I think I now know what that is—I can only do it with her approval. Whatever I might have thought about loving her doesn't work anymore. I have been, and always shall be, her friend, like Mr. Spock said to Capt. Kirk.

But as she gets close and I see her face, I don't think she's thinking of Mr. Spock.

Or being my friend.

She's not smiling, either.

Her mouth is pulled back in a snarl, her face is red, and her hands are balled up into tight fists. My smile drops a little and I feel a little nervous laugh escape between my lips as I take a small step backward, thinking she's going to stop right in front of me.

Except she doesn't.

She opens her hands at the last second and runs right into me, pushing me hard. I land hard on my butt, scraping my elbows and my hands. I'm like Lily and the others now, where I can feel the torn skin and the blood start to seep out of both elbows and the palm of one hand but it doesn't hurt.

It doesn't feel anything.

It's her face as she stands over me, so angry and hurt, and then her shouting at me, that's what really stings.

"Where have you been, you stupid asshole? How could you leave me alone to deal with Lily and all this shit? How could you leave your mom and dad and put them through that, when they needed you so much after Sara died?"

She stops to take a quick breath, pulling it in sharp through her mouth and into her throat and chest.

"But I—"

"But you what?" she cuts me off, now even more furious that I cut her off. "You've become one of these stupid, whatever they are, like Lily and these two," she motions back at Cameron and Missy who are walking up to us. "I don't give a shit what you are now or what you think your problems are, you don't just run away and—" she gasps, her face knotting all up, "—and leave," she gasps again, her words getting quieter.

Her shoulders shake and she starts to cry. I jump to my feet and step forward, my arms out to hold her, but she jumps back.

"DON'T YOU TOUCH ME! I NEEDED YOU AND YOU WEREN'T THERE! I THOUGHT YOU WERE MY FRIEND!"

Her last word cracks and breaks in her throat from the pressure of her screaming into my face. Her eyes are spilling tears, bright and raging and hurt as she stares at me, wanting something from me, wanting me to be her old and loyal friend, before Lily, before all of this. I close my eyes and drop my head, the good feeling I had about seeing Kathy again, even for a short time, all gone.

I shouldn't have come back. I shouldn't have come back like this and tortured her. If I'm really going to do what I think I have to do, I have to do it alone, I have to take the responsibility by myself. There's no way I can make it right.

Missy comes up to Kathy and puts her arm around her. Kathy breaks down completely into full sobs, her whole body shaking. I just stand there, helpless, as usual. I look at Missy for some help, some guidance, but she has lowered her head and is whispering something in Kathy's ear while stroking her hair.

"You were gone for all of those days," Cameron says, stopping next to Missy. "You left her with the task of burying Lily. You left her with—"

"I know I left her!" I snap at Cameron. "I was scared and I didn't want to be responsible for anybody else dying. I couldn't deal with it!"

"The randomness of this universe, combined with Lily's desire to live a fully human life, killed her, and you had nothing to do with it," he says to me in a stern voice. "She would have died in 10 years or 60 years or at some time in between but she would have died. There is nothing you could have done to help her but you could have stayed to help those still living, like your friends and your family."

His words deflate me, finishing off the job started by Kathy screaming at me. But I can't stand here and feel sorry for myself any more. I did that and left Kathy alone to deal with Lily and everything else. I have to put her needs ahead of mine for a change. I have to—

I remember what I saw while sitting on the bench, before she came. That beaten old machine. I can still hear it, working and chugging and churning. The older man standing at the table, working the dials and handles and knobs, looks tired and frustrated. He's the one waiting for me. I know what he does and I think I know what I should do when I go see him. But putting Kathy and everyone else ahead of me gives me another option, another way out of this, something Amara could never have thought of, never have known. I don't have time to think about it more. Kathy is waiting for me to say something, to give her some answers.

"Kathy," I start, standing where I am and resisting the urge to go to her and hug her. "I'm sorry for leaving you when you needed me. I'm still your friend and you're the only real friend I have left and I left you at the worst time. I could go back and fix it but I don't think that would be the right thing to do."

Kathy looks up at me but doesn't move out of Missy's arms. Her face is streaked with her tears and her eyes are so hurt but she's trying to come back, that practical side of her, that caring side of her. She's curious about what happened to me, where I was. She's wondering if I'm okay.

"What do you mean you could go back and fix it? Like go back in time?" she asks, squinting at me, trying to understand. "What's wrong with you?."

I hold out my hands to the side and just shrug helplessly. There's so much to tell her and I don't know how to do it or where to start, especially when I'm just starting to figure it out myself.

Kathy looks at me now for answers and I just shake my head back at her.

"I'm still trying to get what's happening and what it all means," I tell her.

Kathy fully faces me now and glares at me.

"You'd like to know what's happening and what it

means? Really?" Her voice is sharp and annoyed. I know this voice and this Kathy. She's had it for years and she perfected it in high school. She uses it to cut through my crap and ask me what the hell I'm doing, why I'm being such a jerk. It's not like she had to use it on me that often before but she's never been afraid to use it, either. And now she's waiting for me to answer.

"I know I owe you a lot of explanations since Lily died and—"

"And before that," she cuts in.

"And before that," I nod. "I'll tell you everything I know. Wait, I'll even do better than that."

I hold out my hand to her.

"Come with me and I'll show you."

Before Kathy can move or answer, both Cameron and Missy step forward to each side of Kathy, as if to protect her. Protect her from me?

"No!" Missy shouts, taking Kathy's arm. "That's not allowed!"

"Sam, a human mind is not capable of what you propose. She cannot take that journey with you and remain herself," Cameron tells me in his regular voice but there's a little edge of urgency behind it, like I'm not supposed to be doing something and he's trying to talk me out of it without telling me what I should or shouldn't do.

"But you don't know that for sure, do you?" I ask, staring hard at Cameron and then Missy. "You don't really know what's allowed or not, right? Sure, you know that people go crazy when they see guardians like you guys, but maybe I can bend the rules. Maybe I'm supposed to bend the rules."

Missy just stares back at me before finally looking away, while Cameron bows his head, a small frown on his mouth. I look back at Kathy and step closer, so my hand is easy to reach.

"We don't have to listen to them," I tell her, my voice soft and calm, hoping she can trust me. "You know I'd never hurt you."

She keeps her arms at her side.

"I knew before that you'd never hurt me but I don't know that anymore," she says, her voice low and rough. She's not crying anymore. She's as confused as ever about what to do and what to think, that much I can see in her eyes, but she knows she's hurt and she knows I'm the one who did it.

"Hey, can I come, too?" a voice calls brightly from behind me and there is the sound of shoes clapping on the brick path, running and getting closer.

I turn and there's the little girl, Crocodile, stopping next to me, looking first at me and then the others.

"Hi, there, we haven't met," she says to Kathy, holding out her hand. "My name's Camille. Who are you?"

"Wait!" I yell, stepping forward but too late to stop Kathy from taking the little girl's hand.

"I'm Kathy," she says, smiling. They shake hands and then let go, both of them looking at me weird.

"What's wrong, Sam?" Kathy asks.

"Yeah, we were just shaking hands, you big doofus," Camille says, smiling sweetly at me. "What did you think was going to happen?"

I hold up my hands apologetically.

"Nothing's wrong. Nothing."

"That's not true," Crocodile says, pointing at me. "You've got a job to do and places to be and people to see and that's why I'm here. It's time for you to get going, mister."

See you soon (Missy)

Sam ignores the rest of us, even Camille, and asks Kathy again if she'll trust him and go see who he is and what's really been going on. I hate the idea because I think she'll go bonkers the second Sam takes her wherever he's going to take her and shows her whatever he's going to show her about himself or Lily. I'm surprised she's not loony tunes already with all the stuff she already knows.

But I let go of her arm because I can tell she wants to go. She's too curious. Lily left behind so many questions and even the few answers she left just led to more questions, so now Kathy has to know more. Not giving her answers is what would really drive her over the bend now. Plus, even though she's really mad and hurt, Kathy still trusts Sam. I hope he knows what he's doing this time because he's been pretty unreliable before and he always has these good intentions and then somebody gets hurt or killed and he feels bad about it later but that doesn't seem to stop him from trying again.

So she takes his hand and Camille takes his other hand and you can tell she's pretty happy and then they're gone.

"Cam, what did Camille mean when she said to Sam that it was time for him to go?" I turn and ask him.

He's rubbing his jaw and his mouth roughly with his right hand, like he's trying to squeeze answers out of his face and pull them out of his mouth.

"I do not know, Missy" he says, dropping his hand to his side. "Is it time for him to go and do what Amara crafted him to do or is it time for him to die because he has not done what he was supposed to do in the time available to him? I cannot say. All I know is that I don't believe we shall have to wait long for an answer."

We stand there quietly for a minute. The city streets

are waking up and getting noisier and busier.

"I can still feel them, well, Sam and Kathy anyway, but I wouldn't know how to find them," I say as much to myself as to Cam. "I guess they've gone back in time."

"Or somewhere else," Cam smiles at me, holding out his hand.

"What somewhere else?" I ask, taking his hand and we start walking out of the park and towards the downtown streets. "What do you mean?"

"Have you not ever wondered about what might be beyond what we can see and feel, what is beyond the borders of this universe?" he asks, squeezing my hand. His white cane is tap-tap-tapping in front of us.

"Sure, we all have, and there's nothing there, nothing at all, no energy, nothing moving, nothing, you know, being," I answer. "That's a Bodie way of thinking about things, always wondering what's past his own nose."

"It's also a human way of thinking, my dear, but that does not mean it is without merit," he says, as we reach the crosswalk and he stops. "I do not see the white lines in the roadway here, visually telling me that this is a safe place to cross on foot, but you once told me they were there and I believe you. It seems to me that Sam is now aware of paths, crosswalks, that we are not. Do we trust him if he tells us they are there? Do we trust him to lead us across to safety, to somewhere else, the same way I put my trust in you?"

There aren't any cars coming so I lead him across the road.

"So does that mean anything could happen, things we won't even understand, because we can't see them?" I ask. "Where are we going, anyway?"

"Just because Sam sees other options does not suggest

even he knows our final outcome but I suspect Camille may know, in her own way, what is ahead for him," he answers, turning left. "All I know is what is ahead for us."

"What's that, Cam?" I say, looking around nervously since I have no idea what's ahead for us.

He takes a deep breath through his nose, sniffing the air.

"Breakfast," he says, smiling.

"Okay," I say, seeing the sign outside a coffee shop advertising their morning meal specials. "How about this place we're coming up to right here?"

Cam doesn't answer me and we end up walking right by the front door. It does smell pretty good so I bet the food would be really tasty.

"Cam?"

"Take me north on Water Street," he answers finally. He was walking but it was like he wasn't even here for a few seconds. "It is just ahead of us, I believe. Lead me to the tallest building down by the water."

"No breakfast?" I ask, a little sad.

"No, Missy," he pats my hand. "Sam just spoke to me and he wants us to meet him there."

"He spoke to you? Did he say why we have to go there?" I ask.

"No, but he did say we'll know what to do when we get there," Cam says. "No, Missy, I don't know what he means," he adds, before I can ask.

"Well, I hope we can have breakfast there," I say, turning us left to walk across the street and down the side-walk. I can see the building Sam must mean from here.

"I hope so, too," he nods.

The long walk (Kathy)

Sam insists on being in the middle, holding my hand and Camille's with his other. I don't know how he's holding Camille hand but he's got a death grip on mine and I'm about to complain about it, tell him to take it easy, it's not like I'm going to let him run away again. We've started walking away from downtown and towards the bridge.

"Okay, Kathy," he turns to me. "Things are going to change, you're going to see the impossible but you're with me so you're safe, okay?"

"You're kidding me, right?" I snap back. "Things have changed and I have seen the impossible already with what Lily—"

I stop talking. Okanagan Lake to our right, the grass and trees of City Park to our left and the path in front of us, leading to the children's water park just ahead, all of it fades out and disappears in a couple of seconds. We're still walking slowly but we're completely surrounded, on the sides, above and below, by nothing but a fog the colour of tea with milk in it, this gross brown colour.

"Let's start in the beginning," Sam says. "And the beginning is with Lily. We'll get to me in a little bit."

"And the beginning is me, too," Camille pipes up beside me.

"And you, too, of course," Sam looks down and smiles at her. He seems to know her well and his smile is big and caring.

The fog slowly starts to move and then, without a sound, all of it is drawn into a single, tiny point right in front of us, like someone is on the other end sucking it up with a straw. Before I can see what's around us, the tiny point shakes for a second and then bursts out, surrounding us with darkness and it's rushing outwards in every direction, chased by a rainbow of colourful clouds and light.

And there are things alive, too. Most of them don't have a shape but I can still see them somehow and I see a dark shape that reminds me of Camille and—

"There I am!" she shouts in excitement, pointing at what I saw. "See me? There I am! I'm all brand new!"

But there are three shapes that really have my attention. Lily is clearly recognizable as human but she's not quite solid yet and she's dancing with Cindy, who is in a solid human shape, except they don't have any clothes on yet. And next to them, off to the side, without a real shape yet, is Bodie, Lily's dad. Further off to the right and behind Bodie, I can barely make them out but there are Missy and Cameron.

"This is the beginning and that was the Big Bang. That's how old Lily and all the rest of the guardians are," Sam says.

"We are aspects of creation, em…um…embodiments of the processes of action and the funk…um…the functioning universe," Camille announces.

"Did Bodie tell you that?" Sam chuckles, looking down at her again.

"Of course Mr. Bodie told me that, silly," she laughs back. "That's pretty neat that I remembered it."

"But what does it mean?" I ask both of them.

"Well, how should I know but it sounds nice and important, right?" Camille answers.

"It means that guardians have been around from the beginning and that's all that you really need to know," Sam says to me.

"But what about—?" I start to ask but Sam cuts me off.

"I'd like to show you more but I'm in a bit of a rush," he says and already the scene is fading and a new time is coming, again with Lily and Cindy. "Like Camille said, I have to go."

I try to stop my feet from moving but there is nothing for them to push against. I still have my voice, though.

"Still about you, isn't it? I'm in a rush. I have to go," I complain. "You're not showing me this to make me feel better, you're showing it to me to make you feel better."

That gets him to slow down but I keep talking.

"And I don't want to see this stuff about Lily and her and Cindy killing those people. I know that and I don't need to see why because I don't care. I just need to know how you got pulled into this and why you're still here doing this."

That makes him stop. Everything stops around us, too, and I look at the snapshot. A group of guardians are attacking Cindy. Instead of rushing to help her, Lily looks like she's flirting with another guardian who seems happy about what's happening to Cindy. I open my mouth to ask what's going on and then close it. I just told Sam I didn't want Lily's history, so I can't be asking.

"Okay, quick story," Sam says, talking faster, his voice tight and sharp, like I know how he gets when he's under pressure to do something he doesn't want to do and do it fast. "Lily kills that guardian she's with, to make the others stop killing Cindy and to stop that guardian from destroying all life in the universe. Lily and Cindy come to live among humans to hide from the killed guardian's friends."

Now we're back in Kelowna, standing in the dark living room of Lily and Cindy's house. Outside, I hear car doors being slammed shut and raised voices but Sam is talking over them.

"Lily and Cindy moved constantly because their bodies didn't age and nobody figured out they weren't human, except for four people who seemed to be able to sense who they were. Those are the four they killed, to avoid being detected by the guardians looking for them. Here's the fifth they killed," he says as the door opens and Sam comes in, following closely by Cindy, who grabs him and with impossible speed and strength, pins Sam up against the far wall, while Lily comes after, calmly closing the door. She looks sad but she's not upset.

"What do you mean the fifth they killed? That's you," I whisper as if they can hear me, forgetting that they can't, since this happened before.

"Listen," Sam says back, squeezing my hand. I've missed some things that were said.

Lily has walked up to where they are and is standing next to Cindy.

"Cindy, why are you hurting me?" Sam moans after Lily touches him on the forehead.

"Because you're an abomination," Cindy growls.

"Don't call him that," Lily says back, angry at Cindy.

"It's what he is. Isn't that right, Sam?" Cindy says, a mean and cruel sound I never heard in her voice in the time I knew her.

"Stop," Sam whines, unable to move. "What's she talking about, Lily? What is this?"

"I'm afraid we're long past questions, boy," Cindy answers. "Your vision is a threat to us and we cannot allow it. I am doing this for your own good. Your madness is already taking over and then you will attract the others. That must not happen."

"But—" Sam is staring at Lily, confused and scared.

Lily puts her head down, leaving her hand on Cindy's shoulder.

Cindy's right hand drives into Sam's chest. Even in the dark, it looks horrible and there's blood everywhere, somehow even darker than the night around us.

"Oh, Jesus Christ," I cry, looking down and covering my face with my left hand. "Why did you have to—"

Sam squeezes my hand again.

"Look," he commands. "Just watch."

I look back and Cindy has stepped back, holding her hand like she's hurt, and Lily's hands are in Sam's chest and she pulls out his heart and it stops beating in her hand but he's still standing there, still alive.

"Don't worry, she gave it back to me, not once but twice," Sam says next to me, sounding a little sad and we're moving forward again, now to a beach along Okanagan Lake, and there's Sam, bringing his heart back to life and giving it to Camille, who takes it like she's never seen anything so beautiful or perfect, before running off down the beach.

"I still have it for you, Sam, and it's beating and everything, right here in my little purse, for when you need it and I think you need it pretty soon, right?" Camille says, her voice still bright but sounding more serious.

Sam turns to her but is too shocked to say anything. He wasn't expecting that.

"I'm not sure how yet, either, but I think you're probably right," Sam finally answers, sounding tired and confused.

We're in an elevator now and it's going up. Sam lets go of my hand and Camille's hand but turns to me.

"I think that's because this is where I'm supposed to be. We're back in our time now but we're going to a place no other guardian knows about, no other guardian has ever seen," Sam says, speaking low.

"I knew about it, sorta, but I didn't know how to get here," Camille says cheerfully as the elevator slows down. "I knew Sam would have to take me here one day, I knew he would."

We all face the door as the elevator stops and a light bell rings.

"What is this place?" I whisper to Sam.

He closes his eyes as the doors start to open. He's shaking and I suddenly realize how scared he is.

"This is where everybody dies!" Camille shouts happily, running through the doors before they're even finished opening.

Lights out (Amara)

I am alone, standing on a beach in my human form in the full light of day. The others have no doubt scattered as far as physically possible from this place but they are of no consequence. Cameron and Missy are close, still in Kelowna, but I could not say precisely where they are or what they are doing.

Sam and Camille are not nearby, either. They were both close and then suddenly, abruptly, they were both gone. I resist going to look for them because what would I say or what would I do when I found them? Beg them to end my existence now? It is what I want but I will not beg for it, otherwise it will have no meaning. I am still convinced Sam's human self is quickly wearing away and the power I invested in him will be used as I intended.

I am also convinced I will not have long to wait.

But if I have to wait, I shall do so in my truest form

so I leave my human form and embrace the light, drawing comfort in its speed, its warmth and its diversity. Before I have time to fully integrate myself, however, I suddenly feel Sam everywhere, all around me. His voice is inside of me, speaking gently but with authority.

"Amara, it's time. I'm ready. I need you to light the way for the others."

I try to speak back to him, tell him how much I love him, how much I'm willing to serve him in these last moments, but he has already departed. I see my task. Sam and Camille are in a place I never knew existed before this moment. I am unable to see them yet but they are in a physical space at the top of a tall building that looms over the city, and I can see that Sam needs me to be his beacon, to show all of us guardians the path to him.

So I let myself fully dissipate, spreading my light to the furthest reaches of our existence, while keeping a burst of my essence to shine on the base of the building, the door that is the final exit from this place. Cameron and Missy are the first ones there, getting there just as I do. They stop and wait at the bottom by the door, the entrance to where Sam waits. Missy smiles and waves to me, while Cameron simply turns his face up and basks in my brightness, the glimmer sparkling from his dark sunglasses, a look of satisfaction across his mouth.

The first guardians arrive, many of them abstract but some of them in human form, and they are greeted warmly by both Missy and Cameron, before being shown through the door, where they disappear and are taken to where Sam and Camille await. The door opens again in a few moments and the next guardians are directed inside. They all look so relieved, that this is finally happening, that they finally get to rest. Sam has spoken to all of them as well, I presume, and they finally believe me.

And so it goes for the entire day, until finally, in the early evening, there are no more guardians waiting. As the door closes on the last of them, Missy beckons me to come down to them, waving broadly with her arm. I decide at the last moment to take human shape, to stand with Missy and Cameron, but mostly so I can be in the same form as Sam for the last time that he sees me.

"Greetings, Amara, my sister," Cameron hails me formally, nodding his head and bowing slightly, his arms out to his side.

"Hi, Amara, my sister," Missy adds, also greeting me respectfully but her bow is much quicker and clumsier than Cameron's. "That's a really nice necklace you have on."

"Greetings to you both, Cameron, my brother, and Misery, my sister," I respond in the formal fashion, smiling at both of them and bowing twice, once to each of them. "Thank you for the compliment. Camille asked me to carry Devi's essence and this is what remains of her."

"I apologize that you are left with that burden," Cameron says.

"No apology is required because it is no burden," I smile at him. "I am flattered that Camille left me to carry Devi's essence to the end."

There is the sound of a bell and the door opens quietly. The three of us turn and face it. It sits quietly, waiting for us to enter.

"Do you wanna go first, Amara?" Missy asks, looking back at me.

"No, let us all go together, the three of us," I respond, holding out my hand and motioning them towards the elevator.

Cameron goes into the elevator first, his cane tapping

the floor and then the metal frame and the dark wood interior, finding its perimeter and where to stand. Missy joins him, taking his arm with her hand. They have both turned and are facing the front as I come inside with them. I do not face the front but turn sideways to face the two of them as the doors quietly slide shut and we begin moving upwards. There are no buttons to press on either side of the doors and there are no numbers above the doors to indicate where we are going or how close we are to our destination.

"It appears that you have accomplished your goal, Amara. My congratulations to you on your perseverance," Cameron speaks, without turning in my direction. His voice is soft and sincere.

"Yeah, congratulations," Missy mutters.

"Missy," Cameron lightly pokes her with his elbow. "This is how things are. This is how things must be. We talked about this."

"I know, I know," Missy's head droops for a moment before she raises it, looking at me. "I'm happy for you, Amara, I really am. I just don't feel very happy for me, that's all."

I cannot restrain my laughter and it sounds tingly and metallic even to my ears as it comes out of my throat. It still makes Cameron smile.

"What's so funny, you guys?" Missy's head goes back and forth between us, a pout already on her face. "I didn't say that to be funny. It's true!"

"Missy," Cameron gently tells her. "Here at the end, how else would you feel but what is in your nature? How else would you feel except miserable?"

Missy tightens her mouth to think about what Cameron has said and he is right, of course. He is not

Bodie but Cameron knows many things. She glares at the door and stands quiet.

"Thank you for your kind words, both of you," I finally say. "You both have been with me for small but significant parts of my journey and, while I did not appreciate your company at the time, I am grateful for it, nonetheless."

"I should have stopped you when I had the chance," Missy grumbles.

Before either I or Cameron can respond, the elevator slows and comes to a smooth stop, accompanied by the ringing bell.

"Our final destination," I smile as the door opens.

Before the doors have fully parted, we all hear the sound of destruction. Items made of glass and wood and metal are being smashed in anger, quickly and forcefully. The lights in the elevator go out as the doors finish opening. There is only one source of light ahead of us, a small candle with a delicate but resilient flame, that still manages to fill the small room.

The smashing stops and a figure, with its back to us, standing in shadow in front of a table that fills more than half of the room, beckons us with his hand.

"Get in here, you guys," Sam growls, "before the elevator disappears."

The three of us step forward as one into the room without hesitation. Behind us, there is a groaning sound and where the elevator once was, there is now only a wall.

"Yay, you did it, you big old alligator! Great job!" Camille shouts enthusiastically. I had not seen her until she spoke but she is standing at Sam's side, also with her back to us, up on her toes so she can see what's on the table. "You just have a little bit more to do and then you're all done!"

"I know, I know," Sam says wearily, his shoulders slumped. He takes a deep breath, pulling himself up straight and turning around. "We have some last visitors to deal with first."

"Oh, it's you guys," Camille turns to face us. "This better not take long."

"It won't take long at all, little crocodile," Sam smiles, rubbing the top of Camille's head with his hand.

She turns toward us, as well, smiling and looking up at Sam with admiration.

"I need you to keep Missy and Cameron company for just a minute while I have a chat with Amara, okay?" he says, bending down to her height.

"You got it, good buddy," she says, nodding assertively.

Sam straightens up to his full height and looks at me. He says nothing for a moment and I just stare back at him, admiring my creation. He is everything I had hoped for. Finally, Sam smiles slightly.

"Amara, could you come here, please? There's something I need to show you," he says, holding out his hand for me to take.

I take it and he brings me up to the table.

"What do you see?" he asks me, motioning to the table.

I walk up to its edge. I cannot recognize what could have been here before because everything has been smashed into so many pieces, so thoroughly, that there is nothing but fragments. I look at Sam, wondering what it is he wants me to see. He is watching me.

"Look again, look carefully," he urges, tilting his head.

I obey Sam's wishes, carefully analyzing the contents of the table from where I stand. I notice not a single piece has fallen off the table and touched the floor but before I can ask how or why that is so, I see a small glass vial, unbroken, on the right side of the table. It looks like there is nothing in it but I can feel it from here, now that I see it, now that I know it is here.

I look at Sam, confused. He knows that I saw it and a small smile has crossed his face. I do not like it.

"Everything is gone, everyone, well, almost everyone, is dead, just like you wanted, just like Camille wanted. There's nothing left anywhere, except for what's in this room and that little thing I left for you on the table," he tells me.

I lunge for it but he easily catches my hand and his grip is strong. I try to escape my physical form but I cannot. His hold on me is thorough. I continue to struggle, regardless, staring only at Samael, the real Samael, contained and trapped. If I could only release him, he would finish this for always and I could be with him.

"Amara," Sam says to me in a quiet voice as everything in the room, the table, the others, even the physical form of Sam, slips away. We are in the dark and Sam lets go of me. "We're here. He's here."

And then I feel my true love and I let my unpure physical self evaporate and my light be free. It is nothing. It is insignificant in the dark. Sam is gone, everything is gone, and I am here with my Samael and he surrounds me and caresses me and everything is perfect. I say nothing and he says nothing. I just reach out further and further until I feel a breaking point, when I will not be able to draw my essence back together, when I will be completely lost in the dark.

I push through.

Lights out (Missy)

"That was most gracious and kind of you," Cameron

says to Sam when he comes back and Amara isn't with him.

When the two of them are together, I have to call him Cameron because the names are too close. Cam and Sam. And now there's Camille. I bet if we were really friends, I'd call her Cam, too, but no, I wouldn't because that would be really messed up. Cam and Cam and Sam. I shake my head, trying to stop my brain from spinning off like this. Cameron, Camille and Sam.

Sam shrugs his shoulders and hands the little glass tube from the table to Camille. She turns it around and around in her hands, her face scrunched up, then hands it back.

"Why you giving me this? I don't want it," she says, annoyed.

Sam takes it.

"Just wondering…you know…if you want to…take care of it," he says.

"Hey, mister, I've been doing my job a lot longer than you," she crosses her arms. "You have to do it. I'm just the one who has to be there. Mr. Bodie said I'm the witless, I mean the witness. I can't do it. So you do it and then there ain't nobody here but us chickens."

We all laugh, especially me, because I'm completely relaxed now that Amara has gone. As soon as she disappeared with Sam, I just felt this whole tension leave. I tried to be nice to her at the end but it was hard. I just didn't like her much. She was mean and cruel—always talking all fancy and smiling didn't change that for me. I'm still laughing at Camille's joke but also thinking about all this stuff with Amara when Sam turns back to the table and throws down the glass tube, breaking it into a zillion pieces.

The sound is horrible, it's so sharp and painful. I scoot over to Cameron, grabbing his arm. I think I even whimper a little. Cameron tries to bring his hands up to cover his ears but he's too late. He turns his head and his face twists up, all hurt. The sound fades slowly but not fast enough. It sounds wild and hurt, like a wounded animal trapped down a deep well.

"How was that?" Sam says at Cameron, not laughing any more. "Was that gracious and kind?"

"Not to me or Missy," he answers. "But it was what Amara wanted and you made it a gift, one she could never have even imagined."

"A gift? That wasn't a gift. I reunited her with all that was left of Samael from a moment in time and then killed them," Sam answers all huffy, his nostrils flaring. "That was cruel, don't you think? Giving her what she always wanted and then destroying her, too—that doesn't seem too great to me."

"No, I do not think that was cruel, Sam," Cameron says, standing up straight and sure of himself. "Camille is not the only one who has been doing her job for a very long time. I know what forgiveness is and I know you forgave her and I admire you for that. You not only granted her deepest wish but you reunited her with her love at the same time. You did not have to do that for her but you still did."

Sam looks down and away, shaking his head in disgust. He might have done this nice thing Cameron says he did but I don't think Sam's very happy that he did it.

"She didn't deserve it. She killed Cindy. She made me into…this," he says, looking at his hands and down at his body.

Cameron walks up to him slowly and I come with

Cameron. I start to understand a little better why we're here at the end of things, the three of us with him. Sam is shutting everything down, closing up the shop, because that's what he was made to do, so that's why Camille is here. And he feels horrible about it, hates himself for it, which is why I'm here. And he somehow forgave Amara for putting him in this position, which is why Cameron is here. But that can't be right. That's not enough. There has to be more to it. He's finding a way to forgive himself for doing what he's doing. I concentrate on what Cameron's saying. He's reaching out to touch Sam's arm.

"I could not agree more that she did not deserve it, which is what makes what you did a true act of kindness and forgiveness," he says gently. "She made you to do what you've done, she made you to destroy her and everything else but she never imagined you would reunite her with Samael before you did. Even she didn't understand the power she left you."

"If Lily forgave her, then I had to, too," Sam looks at Cameron, pain in his face.

Now I leave Cameron's side and go to Sam. I don't say anything. I just put my arms around him and he takes me into his arms, squeezing. I pat the back of his head and neck.

"Lily forgave Amara for killing Cindy and Amara forgave Lily for killing Samael," Cameron explains. "That does not mean they became great friends or that they even liked each other. But they understood each other. You were under no obligation to forgive Amara for creating you, for giving you your power, but you have."

I let Sam go and I take his face into my hands, forcing him to look at me.

"You feel at peace with yourself and hate yourself at

the same time for what you've done," I tell him, more forcefully than I mean to but part of it is to tell him and part of it is me trying to understand it. "That's why me and Cam are still here, I get that. All the other guardians are dead, everything living in the universe is dead, all the people, your parents, your friends, Kathy—"

Sam takes my hands into his and pulls them off his face.

"I didn't kill Kathy, Missy," she says, stepping to the side slightly so I can see better the table and how smashed and wrecked everything on it is.

"She made up her own mind and chose to go," Camille says, standing on the other side of me. "She took the maintenance man with her."

"What?" I say, looking at Camille, then back at Sam. Now I'm really confused.

"Who is this 'maintenance man' you speak of, Camille?" Cameron asks and I can hear in his voice he's pretty confused, too.

"How should I know? I had never met him before we got here" Camille says, shrugging with her hands out. "That's what he called himself, anyway."

"I can explain, I think," Sam says. "The maintenance man, Max,"

"Right, right," she says, snapping her fingers. "Max, that's his name. Max, the maintenance man."

She looks back at Cameron.

"You know, he's the guy I told you about, you know the one I could feel when Lily…um… went away," she says, looking down at her feet. She doesn't want to upset Sam so she doesn't even say that Lily died.

"It's okay, Crocodile.

Sam shrugs his shoulders.

"I couldn't see him before and even you guys couldn't see him because he was behind the scenes, behind the curtain, keeping things... well, maintained, I guess," Sam says, then he holds his arm out over the table. "Well, it was maintained until I got here."

"You killed the creator?" I shout in disbelief.

Camille answers before Sam has a chance.

"Oh, don't be such a silly," she says, smacking me on the arm and startling me. "Max was the maintenance man, remember? It was his job to keep things running. He didn't create nothing."

"But he is gone?" Cameron asks.

"Duh," Camille answers. "Yeah."

"And Sam, you have destroyed what he was maintaining?" Cameron says to Sam, ignoring Camille's insult.

"Well, I'm not going to say 'Duh' again but I think that's pretty obvious, don't you?" Sam answers, then he takes on a fake, deep voice, like a TV announcer. "Sam Gardner, universe destroyer."

Cameron shakes his head, still puzzled. He strokes his chin.

"So what happens now?" I blurt out.

Sam holds out his hands, one to me and one to Cameron.

"What do you think?" he answers, smiling at both of us.

Camille starts a little dance beside me.

"Oh," I answer quiet, looking at Cameron and then back at Sam. I guess it's time.

"But before you go with Camille, I want to show you something and you won't have to take my word for it," Sam says.

"What's that?" I say.

"Take my hand, Missy," he answers.

I reach out and grab Cameron's hand, squeezing hard, and then I take Sam's hand.

"I'm glad you're here with me at the end, Cam," I say, standing straight.

Cameron reaches forward to take Sam's hand.

"I do not believe this is quite the end yet, my dear," he says, squeezing my hand back.

Before I can ask what's going on, the room starts to change. The last thing I hear is a little girl's voice.

"I'll wait here until you bring Stupid and Mr. Cameron back," she says.

Maxwell's silver hammer (Kathy)

Sam is holding my hand and we walk through the doors into a single room with no other doors or windows. The room is about the size of the living room at home but the only thing here is a huge table that covers most of the room. The only light is coming from the table itself and there are sounds coming from it, too, the sounds of things moving and grinding and turning.

"Stop right there, young lady!" an older man standing on the far side of the table shouts at Camille, his hands up in the air.

Camille was nearly at the edge of the table but stops dead in her tracks, staring in shock at the man now striding around the table towards her. Sam leads us up to stand behind Camille as the man comes up to us, glaring at Camille.

"You keep your dirty hands to yourself, you brat!" he growls at Camille, who backs up into Sam and then turns and hugs him, burying her face into his shirt.

"And you!" he raises an accusing finger in Sam's face. "I know why you're here and it's about time but you're not supposed to bring her here until I'm gone."

Sam's hand is on Camille's shoulder protectively.

"I'm…uh…I'm sorry," Sam manages to spit out.

The man seems younger now that he's closer. His grey hair is thick on his head and combed stylishly to one side in a wave. He's wearing blue jeans and a black and white tartan shirt, with the sleeves rolled up to his elbows, showing his thick and hairy forearms. He's thin but strong, all muscle and not a stitch of fat on his body. He looks like he could snap any of us in two. His clean-shaven face is really familiar to me, his eyes sharp and attentive.

He sees me staring at him and the anger evaporates from his face, his eyes turning soft and his face exploding into a broad smile, centred with perfect straight and shiny teeth.

"Please forgive my rude welcome to these two," he holds out his broad hand to me. "I am so pleased, however, to see you. My name is Max and I am the maintenance man. I am most honoured to be in the presence of one of the children of Bodie and Cindy."

Not sure how I ended up as one of Bodie and Cindy's kids. Is he mistaking me for Lily somehow? He bows his head respectfully and I take his hand. He does nothing more than give it a gentle squeeze and it hits me so hard that I can't breathe. Every muscle in my body is frozen but my brain is spinning in freefall. I don't know where I am, I don't know what this is, but this is impossible but there he is, an older, more mature and wiser version of Sam standing in front of me, holding my hand just like the young Sam is standing beside me, holding my other hand.

"Sam," he says, looking away from me to him but not letting go of my hand. "please allow me a moment to speak privately with your friend. I ask that you and," he glances down at Camille and his lip curls in disgust, "your little companion keep your hands to yourself for the moment."

Without asking for my permission, he starts to lead me to the other side of the room, where he had been standing when we first came in. I let go of Sam's hand quickly and follow Max, gripping his hand tight. He's more than old enough to be my dad but I'm immediately drawn to him and his energy. He's not really Sam but he's how I always thought Sam should be, sure and confident.

"What is your name, young lady?" he says, pulling me alongside him as we walk along the side of the table, approaching the corner.

"I'm Kathy," I breathe, flirting shamelessly but unable to help myself. "I'm pleased to meet you, Max."

We're now on the opposite side of the table from Camille and Sam. Camille has turned around to look at us but she's still pressed against Sam, who has his hands on her shoulders. She's staring at Max with so much hatred in her eyes that it takes me off guard. She's not just annoyed at Max for yelling at her. She hates him with every bone in her body but she's also terrified of him. I want to call across the table to her, ask her what's wrong, why she's behaving like this, when Max starts talking to me, taking all of my attention.

"Kathy, I am not who you think I am," he says, staring deep into my eyes, pleading for my understanding. "I am…a relative, if you will, of Sam's, but I am not Sam."

"Okay," I murmur, feeling my face get red and hot with embarrassment at how see-through I am. "Well, who are you, really, and what is this place?"

His mouth turns into a kinder smile.

"Well, I am Max, I am the maintenance man and this is the maintenance room," he says, holding his hand out over the table. "And this is what I maintain."

I had seen and heard the table when we had first come in but got distracted by Max. I step to the edge of the table and feel like I'm at one of those viewpoints to look into a canyon, except this one doesn't have a railing.

Max takes my right hand in his right hand and stands slightly behind me and to the side, his left hand heavy and strong rests on my left shoulder. Never had a thing for older guys before and never had a love at first sight or any of that crap experience before but Max is blowing all that away. I lean back slightly, so I'm pressed against him, and not just because looking at the table scares me and makes me think I'll fall into it somehow.

"You're safe with me, Kathy," he murmurs into my ear and I believe him absolutely. His breath makes me think of a cedar forest, the trees tall and thick and massive around me. "Look again. Look closely."

I obey him and stare at the table, looking at the things above the surface of it, spinning wheels, clicking gears and pulleys, belts and chains, slackening then tightening, then slackening again. The pieces are tiny and the whole machinery is not tall - the highest piece isn't more than six or eight inches high but it fills the whole table, running right to every edge. It's all connected, all working together, but impossible to follow all at once with so many pieces all moving together. The sound of it is music, beats and tempos all in harmony.

And then I blink and I see what the machine is connected to, everything beneath the surface of the table, the part I'm scared to look at but I feel Max's hands and know I'm safe to see. It's mostly dark but there are small spots of light.

I blink and I get closer to the spots of light, some of them just fuzzy patches, others more defined. I blink again and I'm close enough to see one of the fuzzy patches has colours and shimmers inside, parts of it brighter than other parts. Closer to me is a mostly white ball of light, with some orange in the middle. When I blink again, I can see how there are spiralling white arms spinning out from the white and orange bar at the centre.

"Oh..." I gasp but Max is right here.

"Keep going. You're fine."

The Milky Way is slowly spinning clockwise and I can see and hear the machinery behind it, pushing and pulling it along. I blink and I'm following one of those thin arms, seeing the clusters inside it and then the individual stars inside that and then one star and then an off-white creamy ball near that star.

"That's Venus, my dear," Max chuckles softly.

In the distance, past Venus, I see Earth, a little glittering ball of white, green, blue and brown. When I blink again, I'm close enough to see the moon, a grey pebble beside it, and then the continents and then, closer, the clouds and the oceans and the mountains.

There's a little sliver of a lake, a worm crawling along the ground, and I see Penticton at its bottom, Vernon at its top, and Kelowna in the middle, mostly on the right. With each blink, I'm closer to my hometown, and then my neighbourhood and then my house. And then I'm inside and it's still early because my sister and Mom are still sleeping. I'm in Mom's bedroom now and she's lying curled on her side, with just the sheet on, her hair spread in every direction on the pillow like a fire. I can see her face now, the laugh lines and the worsening condition of her skin as she ages and she looks peaceful, much more relaxed than she does when she's awake and analyzing everything.

"Don't stop," Max whispers. "We're not there yet."

With the next blink, the only thing I can see is the pale land of Mom's skin and then I'm inside, into what must be her brain but there are huge flashes going off everywhere, all around. And the machinery clicks and whirrs even here, the same machinery running the universe and burning the sun and turning the Earth are firing thoughts and dreams in Mom's head. At the cellular level, everything is shaking and vibrating. A few cells slow and then stop but are quickly replaced by new, energized ones, joining in the bond.

Inside the cells are twisting ladders and strings all connected together with these little balls at their centres, branching out in all directions, carrying little sparks of light back and forth. These must be the huge flashes I saw a second ago but they're all just individual tiny points, running along power lines.

And then everything stops making sense. I must be seeing things at the atomic level now or maybe sub-atomic, because now there are huge open spaces with clumps of vibrating matter here and there. Inside the clumps, there is only colour and movement, nothing solid, everything random, confusing chaos. The colours start to fade as we move through the fog and then there is only white but not blinding light, just emptiness. Just nothing at all but I can still hear the machine working.

There, in the distance, is a tiny point, a dot standing out from the white and I move towards it.

"Almost there," Max says. "You're doing great, my dear."

The dot is just black but as I get closer I realize it's not all one colour and there's something inside it, different colours and shapes. I see a room with a big table in the middle and there are two people standing on one side and two people standing on the other. I see my red hair and I fall into the room and before I can stop myself, I fall into my head again. My next blink is the whole table again, with the machinery sitting on top, working away, chattering and clicking in time.

"I can't take credit for creating it," Max says in a soft voice. "I just keep the machinery running."

"It's so beautiful and perfect," I whisper.

"Oh, no, don't be fooled, Kathy. The machinery needs constant care and attention. It wants to break down, it wants to fall apart."

In front of me, a belt falls off of a wheel and gets jammed between some gears. There is a small, whining sound as the wheel scrapes and complains before finally coming to a stop, even though the machinery all around it continues to run.

"Excuse me, Kathy," Max says, letting me go and reaching onto the table, his thin fingers expertly pulling out the belt while holding the gears in place. He quickly hooks the belt up again, tightens it and then sets the wheel spinning again with a quick twist of his finger.

"So you're like the God in the machine or whatever," I say, turning to him.

"I always liked the deus ex machina stories because they were so much closer to the truth than their authors ever intended," he smiles. "Still, the machine doesn't work for me, I work for the machine. It tells me what to do.I think of myself more as the engineer in a cruise ship, working below the decks, keeping the motor running and the boat moving across the water, while everyone above is having a nice holiday and not thinking at all about the engineer below."

"That's a funny way of putting it," I smile back.

His smile fades and he moves closer, leaning his head down so he can speak privately, so Sam and Camille won't be able to hear him over the machinery.

"I will return you to your travelling companions in a moment but I suspect they have not informed you why they are here and what their intent is," he says, his voice low and careful. "Sam is no longer the Sam you once knew and Camille's angelic appearance is a mask for her true role in these proceedings."

"What?" I say, startled, glancing over at Sam and Camille and then I see it. Or I see them not as people anymore.

Sam is just this large mass of black clouds, churning and growling with thunder. He doesn't look like the storm that'll drop a few showers and blow over but the one that'll howl for days and wreck everything you own before moving on. He looms over the table, wanting to descend on the machines and everything. And Camille is besides him, bolts of lightning crackling in all directions, a flash out of the sky that forever changes things. When we got here, when she ran out of the elevator, she said this is where everybody dies. She sounded so happy about it.

I'm a little kid again, frightened of the big storm, and I just want to crawl into bed and pull the covers over my head. Max is close to me again but this time on the other side.

"This is no social call, my dear Kathy. Sam and

Camille are here to destroy all of this. That is why I greeted them the way I did. You should not—"

"Hey, what's going on over there?" Sam shouts and
when I blink, startled by his voice, he's Sam again and
Camille is herself again, too. They both look impatient
and annoyed. "How about coming back here and talking
to all of us?"

Max smoothly takes my left hand and leads me back
around the table on the side we came from, answering
Sam as he walks.

"My apologies to you both for my poor hospitality,"
he says, watching both of them closely. "I was merely
showing Kathy the machinery in closer detail."

"You also showed her something about me!" Sam
yells back. Max seems to be pushing all of his buttons.
"I saw the way she looked at me!"

"I also showed her those who would threaten what I
maintain," Max answers in his same even tone as we stop
in front of Sam and Camille.

Sam holds a hand out for me to take but Max tightens
his hold on my left hand. I shake him off and step to the
side, also ignoring Sam's reach for me.

"You guys can stop talking about me like I'm not here
and I don't like the alpha male thing from either of you
guys. It doesn't suit you," I tell them, my voice louder
than I would like in my ears.

"Sam, why did you take me here? I wanted to know
why you ran away when Lily died, not a grand tour of
the universe."

"He is here to—" Max starts.

"Hey, I let you talk," I stop him. "Now it's his turn."

I can't look at him and be this bossy but I take a quick
glance, anyway. If Max is annoyed with me, he does not

226

show it on the outside. He smiles slightly and nods, crossing his arms in a relaxed way over his chest, then we both turn to Sam, waiting for an answer.

"I didn't want to just tell you, I wanted to show you why I left and what had happened to me because I wanted you…" his voice catches and breaks but he doesn't stop. "I want you… I need you to believe me."

His face bends but he holds it together. His eyes are begging me to understand, to accept him. Normally I would rush to him and give him a big hug and tell him I'll always be there and always trust and believe in him. Now I'm just scared of him, of what's happened to him and what he's seen and done. I see my old Sam but I also see a Sam that left me behind and became something else when I wasn't looking.

Now it's my turn to cross my arms.

"That still doesn't answer my questions, you know," I tell him. "I know you want me to believe you but why? I don't get it. Just tell me."

Before he can answer, Camille stomps forward, her face red and angry.

"You don't get to talk to Sam that way! He doesn't have to listen to you!" she screams at me, her finger wagging up at my face. "I don't have to listen to you, either! This is all so stupid!"

She spins on her heel and takes one step toward the table.

Both Sam and Max move at the same time. They grab her by each arm. She tries to wiggle free, screaming and crying, but they lift her up in the air, so she starts kicking at them.

"Let me go, you jerks! Let me go! You can't do this! You can't!" she wails, having the little kid meltdown.

Max and Sam look at each other, unsure what to do next.

"You're an idiot for bringing her here," Max says, gritting his teeth. "Now what are we supposed to do with her?"

"She's my problem," Sam answers, grabbing Camille with both arms and pulling her away from Max. Sam takes her into a far corner of the room, as far away from us and the table as he can but she doesn't stop yelling and kicking. She's got one arm free and is punching him in the shoulder and the head. Sam abruptly slams her down on her feet and bends down to her height, his hand on his shoulder to keep her in place. His face is right into hers and I hear his words but the sound of it isn't a voice I've ever heard from Sam. It starts low and hard before building up into this rough roar from a deep, dark place.

"You…will…stand…right…here…for a…time out… until I…SAY SO!"

Camille glares at Sam for half a second and then completely falls apart, her hands covering her face and she cries with her whole body. She tries to say a word here and there but nothing comes out that you can understand over her sobs. Sam stands up, straight, turns his back on her and walks over to us.

"I HATE YOU! I HATE ALL OF YOU, ESPECIALLY YOU, ALLIGATOR, YOU BIG MEANIE!" she screams at his back but she doesn't move from her spot and he doesn't turn.

"Did you hear that? I'm a big meanie," Sam smirks at Max and me. "I'll never be the same again."

Max is wrong. This is the Sam I know, putting a bratty kid in her place and then cracking jokes about it. And that smile—you can't copy it and you can't fake it. It's Sam.

I don't care what I saw from across the table. I don't care about what he's done because he had to make a choice in a bad situation. He's still Sam after all this and that's what's important.

"Who's Alligator?" I ask, smiling back at him.

"It's a thing we have," he shrugs back. "See you later, Alligator. In a while, Crocodile. She won't call me Sam and she doesn't like it when I call her by her real name."

I want to ask him more questions, like how long he's known her and what she's doing here and what she really is but Max jumps in.

"Thank you for dealing with her," Max says, nodding his head. "You should have stood up to her a long time ago."

"Maybe," Sam shrugs at Max, then looks over at me. "I don't know what he showed you or told you about me a few minutes ago and I didn't get a chance to show you who I really am and what I've done since I figured out I had this power," he says, staring hard into my eyes. "I killed guardians, the people like Lily and Cindy, because they were hurting me and they were trying to hurt Lily, I killed Sara because she was like me and she attacked me and if I hadn't stopped her, I don't know what would have happened. I like some of what I've done, I hate more of it but I'm not ashamed of what I did and I'm done being scared of what I have to do."

I'm trying to process what he's saying but it's coming too fast. He killed his own sister? He killed other people like Lily and Cindy? How? I thought Sara died in a car accident. Even though I'm so confused, I also see a side of Sam I haven't seen often enough, this side that came out so rarely before. He's not second guessing himself anymore, he might still be nervous and he still might wonder if he's doing the right thing but he's made a decision and he's going to follow through. Now I have to find out what that is exactly. But I don't have to ask. He's already talking.

"I'll answer the stuff about Lily first. I ran away because I was scared and I didn't know what to do. I didn't want to make things any worse. And without Lily to help me think things through, reminding me why I had to kill Sara, I didn't know if I could do it by myself. I needed some time to do that on my own, although I had a friend in Missy who helped me a little."

"But Sam, I'm your friend, why didn't you come to me? We could have helped each other," I cut him off. "I don't understand all this stuff about killing people and killing Sara. That's not right. That's not what happened."

"I...You saw how these people, the guardians, can screw people up, just by showing them who they really are. I didn't want you to go crazy or want you to kill yourself—that's why I couldn't ask for your help," he says, his voice fast and rising. "I've been protecting you ever since we met at the bench, so you would see them in people shape and not their true selves. That's why I didn't like it when Max showed you how I really am, how Camille really is."

"So you could have protected me then, too," I answer, crossing my arms. "You chose to leave because you can't be around people any more. You didn't want your parents or me or anyone else to stop you from doing the thing that made Cindy and Lily scared of you when they tried to kill you and couldn't."

My words are getting slower and my voice is getting quieter because I'm thinking it through as I'm talking and the more I talk, the more I'm realizing what I'm saying and what's really going on.

"I don't believe…you killed people…and I know Sara died… in that accident. I don't believe…why we're here now. How am I supposed to believe…you're going to… wreck the machine…wreck everything…everybody… will die…," I look at Sam, hoping I'm wrong but knowing, feeling that I'm not. I know what I saw when I was on the other side of the table.

Sam can't look at me. He's staring down and away, biting his lip, his jaw all clenched. He's trying to say something, anything, to me but he can't find the words.

Before he can answer, Camille starts clapping her hands loud and slow.

"Way to go, smartypants," she snarls. "You figured it all out. Good for you."

"Sam does not deserve your cruelty for all that he's about to do for you, young lady," Max snaps at Camille. "Kathy has done nothing to you to earn your disdain, either."

Camille looks down at her feet.

"Sorry, Sam," she murmurs. "Sorry, Kathy. That wasn't very nice of me."

Neither of us have time to accept her apology.

"I owe you both an apology," Max says, looking first at Sam than at me. "It should not have been me to inform you, Kathy, of Sam's role here. Sam should have been given the opportunity to tell you himself."

I just stand there, staring at him. I can't think, never mind say anything.

"So I guess I have to do what I have to do," Sam mumbles, staring at the floor in front of him.

"You do," Max answers, so quietly I can barely hear him over the machines on the table.

"So what are you saying? Sam took us here just to kill everybody and wreck your little operation here?" I finally say, holding back my tears.

Max just looks at him and nods, ignoring me. "I'm really tired, Sam, really tired. This thing is falling apart and if you don't fix it soon…"

A high-pitched squeal comes from the corner of the table. Something is making a scraping and grinding sound somewhere else. The noise gets louder.

"I'll do it, Max," Sam reassures him. He's way too calm and it's scaring me.

"No, Sam. No," I can't hold back my tears anymore.

Sam doesn't move. It's Max who comes over to console me, putting his hands on my arms.

"He's doing it because he has to," he tells me. "I can't do it anymore and the machinery is breaking down. He's doing it because it's time."

"What do you mean it's time?" I shake off his hands angrily and step back. "How can there be a time to kill not just everyone you know, your own parents and your friends, but everyone?"

"Everyone, everywhere, everything," Sam says, his voice flat and dull, still staring away. "I bring it all to her, to Crocodile, and like she said when we got here, this is where everybody dies."

"But you can stop this," I shout, running up to Sam and grabbing his arms, shaking him so he'll look at me. "You can make this stop, you don't have to listen to them."

"Remember how we used to talk about growing up and becoming important people, powerful people in important positions who would make important decisions?" he looks at me now, trying to make a connection, hoping I can understand. "What if the only decision left was let everything on that table collapse and die because it doesn't work anymore or to destroy it all and then try to rebuild it, to start it all over again?"

"Is that why you were so scared to come in here?" I ask, wanting to understand, trying to figure out a way to get him to stop talking and thinking like this.

"Yeah," he nods and I can tell he's sure of himself. "But as soon as I saw the table and then you looking into it, seeing all of it, I knew what to do, I knew what I had to do. I'm supposed to wreck it all and then try to put it back together somehow."

"No, Sam, no," I say again. I can't stop crying because I know he's made up his mind. "There has to be another way, a better way. This isn't you. It can't be."

He takes me in his arms and I don't fight him. I feel him stroking my hair.

"I wish there was another way or another Sam, I really wish there was, but I can do this. I can do this because of you and because of Lily," he says softly. "I need you to go with Max because you can't be here when it happens. I don't want you to see me like that. I want this to be your last memory of me, as your friend, always."

He lets me go slowly. I try to hold on but he slips away and Max is right here to hold me, like he did before, holding onto one hand, the other on my shoulder.

"Everything's going to be okay, I promise," Sam smiles at me. "Trust me."

"No, Sam, no," I say one more time but weakly. I've blinked away the tears but I still can't focus on Sam.

"She needs to go now, Sam. I need to go now. You have to let us go," Max says, his voice full of sympathy but urgency, too.

"Kathy," Max then says to me, squeezing my hand, leading me closer to him. "Trust Sam and trust me. I would be honoured to leave this place with you."

"Okay," I answer, feeling suddenly dizzy. I turn my head to look at Max but I can't focus on him either. "I like you, Max, but I don't feel very good."

I feel Max's arms all around me, safe and strong, taking away the feeling that I'm losing it and falling apart. Now I feel what Sam was saying. I feel like everything is going to be alright.

"Goodbye, smartypants," Camille says from close by but I can't see her. She's grabbed my hand and is squeezing it. "I mean that—you really are a smartypants. And goodbye, Max the maintenance man, you did a great job."

Max doesn't answer.

Everything goes black but I hear a sound and it reminds me of a train, coming closer.

Maxwell's demon (Sam)

That was hard to go back and relive that again, to see Kathy so upset and then to see her die but it was the right thing to do. I needed Cameron and Missy to understand what I had done but, most of all, I needed to understand what I did.

Wrecking the machine was easy but I'm going to need Kathy and what she meant to me in my head if I have any chance of rebuilding this stupid thing.

"That is two more acts of generosity and kindness you have committed since you have been here," Cameron says to me as soon as we all take shape again after having gone back to see what happened with Max and Kathy.

Before I can answer, Missy comes and gives me

another big hug.

"That was really awesome of you, Sam," she says, squeezing hard. "Thank you so much."

"Yeah, sure," I answer back, a little startled, instinctively putting my arms around her in return. "No problem, but what was so awesome about it? That wasn't nice to Kathy at all."

She steps back and joins Cameron's side again, taking his arm with her free hand. They're both smiling at me.

"Yes, it was kind to Kathy," Cameron says. "You could have simply destroyed reality and never faced her again but you did. It wasn't the answer she wanted but she did want to see you again, despite what you did. In time, she would have understood and, in the end, she would have accepted who you are and what you are doing. And you had the two of them—Max and Kathy—go together. That was thoughtful."

"That was really sweet of both you and Camille," Missy says, nodding.

"Okay, so we're done, right?" Crocodile says, standing beside me, looking up at me and then, once I look down at her, she glances over at Cameron and Missy. "It's time for all of us to go, right? Them, too?"

"And you, too," I smile back at her, putting my hand on the top of her back, just below her neck and shoulders. "You're all finished, too."

Crocodile breaks out into a huge smile.

"That's great!" she says, her voice bright and happy. "This is a tough job, you know, and I'm getting a little tired, just like Mr. Max."

"You had the most difficult task of all of us, little one," Cameron says. "I do not envy you."

"I don't know what that means," she says back to him.

"But thanks, anyways!"

I bend down on one knee so I'm at Crocodile's height. We look at each other seriously for a moment and then she jumps forward, throwing her arms around me.

"I didn't mean that about hating you, what I said before, you know that, right?" she says, her little hands hanging on tight to my shoulders. "I was just mad and I have a temper, you know."

"It's okay, I know you didn't mean it," I answer, patting her back.

"But, listen," I continue, letting her go. "There's one more thing I need from you, something I gave you and I hope you kept it."

She snorts and then starts fishing inside her little purse.

"Of course I kept it, silly alligator," she says. "I knew you would need it again someday so I kept it right here for safekeeping."

Her little hand struggles to get a grip on it but she finally pulls out my heart, steadying her hold on it with her other hand. Her face is serious in concentration, with her tongue poking out of the side of her mouth, and she's staring at it to make sure she doesn't drop it. It beats slowly but steadily in her hand.

"Oh," Missy gasps. "I wasn't expecting that."

"Neither was I, my dear," Cameron answers.

I hear Missy open her mouth to ask a question but nothing comes out. Instead, I can feel her watching me as I reach forward with both hands and carefully take my heart from Crocodile.

"Whew!" she says, backing away in relief. "I wouldn't want to have dropped that. Not something so valuable and important!"

"But I don't get it," Missy finally blurts out. "I don't

get why it's so valuable and important."

I stand up and stare at my heart, cupped in my hands, the muscle squeezing and relaxing. It is red and vibrant but there's no blood coming from it.

"No more questions, no more questions," Crocodile says, stepping up to Cameron and Missy, holding a hand out to each of them. "Sam's got work to do and he doesn't have time to blah-blah-blah with us."

Cameron pats Missy's hand on her arm and then reaches for Camille.

"Stay with me, my dear friend," he says, turning to Missy with a peaceful look on his face. "I will explain everything."

"Okay, Cam. I'll go wherever you go," she smiles back at him and then reaches out to Crocodile.

I turn away to face the table, partly because I don't want to see them leave and partly because I need to find a place to put my heart for a minute. There isn't a spare space anywhere. The whole area is littered with all the broken pieces. There isn't any movement anywhere, either on the surface of the table or beneath it.

"Well, everything's dead and gone," Crocodile says, standing beside me. "Well, except for you and me, of course, but it's not your turn yet for a really long time and me—"

"Yeah, what about you?" I cut her off, looking down at her. "How do you kill death, anyway? And how can death be living in the first place?"

Before I can flinch, she thumps me on the head hard with Cameron's walking stick. It doesn't hurt but it catches me off guard.

"Don't be such a stupid!" she scolds. "I'm not death, I'm Camille or Crocodile to you. Death is just my job.

Now stop talking and do your job!"

I just look at her. She's staring up at me, expecting me to do something.

"I know what I have to do, I just don't know how to get started," I shrug my shoulders.

"Well, I'm pretty sure you need to put that—" she says, using the stick to point at my heart, still thumping away in my hands, "—back where it belongs," and she taps my chest with the end of the stick.

She takes the stick in her two hands, one on each end, holding it across her body. Then she raises it above her head and brings it down fast. She raises her foot and snaps the stick into two pieces across her upper leg. I've heard the sound it makes before—back when Cindy died. Someone else might have to do the act, like I did with Amara and the remnants of Samael from back in time, or maybe they might surrender to her, like Bodie did and just like Missy and Cameron did now, but nobody really dies until Crocodile is there to see it, to mark it. Max may have been pissed that I brought Crocodile here but she had to come, to be here for his death, and then for the death of everything. He could only let go because I was here. Kathy could only let go because he was there with her.

She chucks the two sticks on the table without a thought, not even looking to see where they land. Then her mouth opens in a huge yawn that she makes no effort to cover, stretching her arms up in the air over her head.

"I'm kinda tired so can you get going?" she says, crossing her arms and tapping her foot.

She looks away and starts whistling a little tune.

I can take a hint. Before I can think about it, I press my heart against my chest, right where Lily's crystal was sitting, hanging from the chain around my neck. I feel this vibration, as my heart first absorbs the chain and crystal, and then, without missing a beat, my heart slides inside my chest, like it was waiting to get back there. I keep my hands pressed against my chest, so I can feel my heart, with Lily part of it, working together, working inside me, pounding away like it's supposed to.

"It's not gonna fall back out or anything, ya know," Crocodile says. "I don't think so, anyways."

"I know," I nod, looking down at my hands still pressed against my chest. "I haven't felt this way in a long time. Like I'm back the way I'm supposed to be. Normal."

"Yeah, whatever," Camille says, ignoring what I said, yawning again. "I really need a nap now, so give me a hug and then tuck me in."

She has her arms open wide to me. I don't worry about the danger or anything because it's just a hug. I bend down on one knee and she moves into my arms. I place one arm across her back and the other across the back of her legs and stand up, holding her tight against me. Her head slumps against my shoulder.

"Now I lay me down to sleep," she whispers in my ear.

"I pray the Lord my soul to keep," I answer back automatically, turning to face the table.

"If I die before I wake," she whispers but now she's slurring her words.

"I pray the Lord my soul to take," I say as I carefully lay her on the table, adjusting her body and then her legs so she's comfortable. She tucks her hands under her head so they make a little pillow and sighs, a little smile across her lips.

"That was pretty funny, wasn't it?" she asks.

"Yeah, that was a good one," I answer.

"See you later, alligator," she murmurs.

"In a while, crocodile," I say, stroking her forehead. "In a long, long while."

She's already asleep and then she starts to fade. I watch her until she's gone, which doesn't take long, but I stare where she was for a few minutes until I can't even imagine her lying there anymore. I look away and blink a few times before looking back to make sure she's really gone. She doesn't exist anymore. She's gone wherever everyone else went when they died and I have no idea where that is. Maybe it's nowhere it all. Maybe she and everything else just stop being. I don't have an answer for that. I just know what's in front of me. There's nothing living except for me and that's all, unless I clean up this big mess and put it all back together.

I'm here at the end of things but the start of things, too. I feel the weight of what I've done but also what I need to do, and it feels so heavy but also light and simple.

How can I make this happen? How can I be the destroyer and the creator, too? It doesn't make complete sense to me but I know it's the truth. Now that I see it, I know I couldn't ever have run from it. Where I was supposed to go and what I was supposed to do was right in front of me. Everything else I did was wrong and I was just putting off what needed to be done. Maybe I could have got away, maybe I could have just turned myself over to Camille but I don't think she'd have taken me and even if I could have made her, I'd just have been forcing someone else, somewhere else, somewhen else, to do what I wouldn't.

I couldn't have handed that off. I couldn't have ignored this.

I had to end the story of this universe, of all the universes. Now I have to start creating the story of a new experience, because this one has run out of time, run out of energy. If I don't do what I'm supposed to do, nothing will live again, all the programs on the computer will stay frozen. That would be worse, much worse, than destroying everything and killing everyone.

I can't let that happen.

So now I'm alone and I snicker at the thought. There's alone and then there's this. There's no one else but me anywhere. There is no anywhere except for here.

"Better get busy then," I say to myself, bending over the table.

I have no real idea what I'm doing or what I'm looking for but then I see two pieces of the machinery that could fit back together. I pick them up, one in each hand, and turn them over, studying them carefully and then, seeing where they could join, slide the one piece into the jagged opening of the other. It gives this clicking sound and now it's in there so good, I can't pull it out. I guess that must be right then. I wonder if there's a wrong way to put this thing together but I don't think so. I have a hunch it's like a puzzle and there's only one way for it to go together.

Now there must be another piece that goes in this spot—there it is, over in the left corner. I go get it and snap that one into place, too, and then put the mechanism down on the table in the space created from picking up the last piece. I grab two small wheels and wrap small round belts inside them before mounting the two wheels, one on each side of the mechanism, adjusting them so that they interlock and one spins with the other. Then I start on two new mechanisms, finding the parts here and there across the table, and once they're done, I fasten the belts from the first device to them.

I catch myself muttering away quite a bit, so after a while I just give up and let my mouth work, putting the thoughts out there, making them real.

"I wonder where that pin could—wait, right here. Ah, there we are. Now if I fasten this piece to that piece, it should—there we go. That's awesome. Okay, now, what about—?" and so on.

I'm either doing that or I'm humming away but there's no song in my head. It's just a background noise, a loose melody not connected to anything. As more of the machinery gets put back together, I can't help but stop and admire my own work. I always sucked at doing models when I was a kid. Dad bought me a few when I was little but gave up when I either glued my fingers together or decided to try to build Transformers out of them but they couldn't be changed back into cars because of the glue. Yet here I am, putting all this together, with no glue, just figuring out how everything fits together and hooking it all up.

I start imagining myself as a mad scientist, a Dr. Frankenstein, bent over his work table, untiring, never stopping for a break, as he pursues his grand vision for creating life. But I'm even better than him. I'm doing it at the universal level and at the sub-atomic level, all at once. I can see it all in front of me, coming closer and closer together, and how it will all lock and fit together. Every shattered piece, which shouldn't be able to be put back together, is finding a place. But there's part of it that feels like I'm pulling things back to the start, separating things that were combined and returning them to the way they began, to their pure state. It's like I'm putting all the spilled milk back in the carton.

As I'm hooking up and reconnecting all the machinery, I'm creating something new while returning everything back to the beginning, to its starting position. I'm not just rewinding the clock. It's a whole new clock now and everything will happen differently. Nothing is certain except for the tension being formed as more and more of the individual mechanisms are being linked together to form one big machine. The belts are tight and the last pieces need to be pushed into place firmly, to hold it all together. There's one last wheel to mount—there—and then this last pin and belt—here—and then stretch over to this wheel—like so—and then...

I'm done.

It's all finished.

I can see all of the separate pieces but everything is joined together into one intricate machine, elaborately woven together, filling up every space on the table, going right out to its very edge. But underneath the table, there's nothing. There's just the beige grey colour of the table.

"So how do I turn it on?" I ask myself out loud.

I circle around the table several times, first one way and then the other, switching directions, now clockwise.

Then I stop and put my hand up to my chest again.

There's one last missing piece. The machine won't work, can't work, without it. I reach into myself and pull out my power. With my heart back in place, all of it leaves me easily and painlessly. I stare down at the black marble in my hand, shaking my head. I wish I could have done that before. I wanted so badly to be able to do it and now, when I don't really want to do it, it pops out of me like nothing, like I just spit it out. I don't really want to give it up, though, because I already feel sorry for the next person who will find this thing inside of them. Someone will find it, I'm sure of that, and then, eventually, they'll find me, too. Someone will come for me. Some day. And when they do, it'll be my turn to die and then the whole thing will start new again.

I toss the marble in the air and it somehow falls through the machinery without touching any of its parts and then falls into the table, a pebble falling into a pond. It's gone for now but it'll get picked up.

For now, its impact is obvious. I can see the wave of sound, spreading across the table, and all at once, everything starts moving, so smoothly and efficiently that a second after it starts, it's hard to imagine what it was like when it wasn't working. Underneath the table, there is a tiny flash and then a whole vision opens up as the universe, pulled back to a single point, wound back up like a spring, releases its energy and starts working again, the machinery holding it all together, channeling that energy into matter and existence.

I stand back for a few minutes and admire how wonderfully it's all working together, listening to the beautiful noise of the gears turning, sounding much better than the racket it was making when I first came in here and it was falling apart since Max couldn't keep up with his maintenance. This is running so perfectly that I doubt I'll ever have to do any...

Wait.

There's a pin loose on the other side of the table. I can hear it vibrating in its slot, clashing with the perfect noise around it, like a C-flat played by one member of the orchestra, when C is the right note. I hustle over and poke the pin back into place. Everything is back as it should be and I stand back again, admiring what is unfolding inside the machine, as the universe starts to take on shapes, gases becoming galaxies, pulled together by strands from the machine, and...

That gear over there is chattering, making the belt vibrate. It's on the other side of the table but I can feel it from here and it's driving me crazy. I have to fix it, so I hustle over and adjust it so that it's running smoothly again, in perfect harmony with everything around it.

And that's how it goes, for the longest time, watching, enjoying and admiring the machine at work, then racing over to fix one thing, adjust something else, back and forth, around the table. There's more things to fix but there's time to watch, to see how things will turn out.

Then I notice Lily, for the first time, and realize she's been there in the machinery all along, since the second just before I threw the marble in the air. She was born from my heart, from my feeling for her, from my wanting to get things working again.

She's not exactly like the Lily I knew but nothing is the same. I have no idea what she's going to do. I have no idea what's going to happen next.

I can see a Bodie and a Cindy, and there's a Missy and a Cameron, too, but it's not really them. Everything's the same but it's different, too. The story is telling itself differently. Amara and Devi and Samael are here, too, but I barely recognize them. If they're going to change, it's going to happen later.

Crocodile is the same but that doesn't surprise me.

I can't stare for too long because there are things to do, little things to fix up so everything runs just the way it's supposed to run.

And I don't really care about the others, anyway. I'm

here looking after things now but Lily is the only one I want to see and follow now.

I keep working and I keep watching her.

I keep noticing everything else happening around her but those are just little details.

The only thing I ever really see is Lily.

The only thing I ever want is her.

Always.

The End.

Resolve

Neil Godbout is the author of Disintegrate and Dissolve, a Prix Aurora finalist for best YA novel from the Canadian Science Fiction and Fantasy Associaton. He lives in central British Columbia, where he is the managing editor of the Prince George Citizen.